TABOOS TROUBLES AND TRUSTS

Tales of football triumph and tribulation

ROB BRADLEY

A donation of £5.00 from the purchase price of this book can be made to a supporters trust of your choice - see rear of book for details

Acknowledgements

One of the aims when writing Taboos Troubles and Trusts was to use local individuals and organisations in its production. Like the subject matter, football, it was intended to be a team effort. A sincere thanks must go therefore to the following admirable people :

Tom and the team at TUCANN*designandprint* for their guidance and workmanship in publishing and producing this book.

Jon Finegold of Keyline Consultancy for editing and proofreading it (www.keyline-consultancy.co.uk).

Grahame Lloyd of Celluloid Ltd for his advice and support.

Andrew Vaughan for the cover photographs.

The Phoenix Players (www.phoenixplayers.org.uk) and local actors Laura Davies, Graham King, Toby Lee, and Gary Burdeau for playing the roles featured on the front and back covers.

Lincoln City fans Steve Buttery and Matt Inglis who also acted their roles so expertly.

First Edition Published in 2010 by TUCANN*books*

ISBN 978-1-907516-08-5

Text © Rob Bradley 2010.
Design © TUCANN*books* 2010
All stories in this volume are works of fiction, and no reference is intended to any person, organisation or football club. All names and businesses are fictitious and any resemblance to any person, living or dead, is coincidental.
All rights reserved. No part of this publication may be reproduced or transmitted in any way or by any means, including electronic storage and retrieval, without prior permission of the author, excpet by a reviewer who wishes to quote brief passages in connection with a review written for insertion in a newspaper, magazine or broadcast.

Produced by: TUCANNdesign&print, 19 High Street, Heighington, Lincoln LN4 1RG
Tel & Fax: 01522 790009 - Website. www.tucann.co.uk

Contents

	Page
Writing Wrongs	7
Man Managing	35
Football Being Football	73
Will Power	98
Relative Success	133
Give and Take	154

About the Author

Rob Bradley has been a football fanatic all his life. His experiences in the game include:

Playing in goal and out-pitch for school and local Saturday and Sunday teams.
Having trials for Boston United reserve team (unsuccessful).
Coaching a cubs team.
Managing a pub team.
Managing a youth side for seven seasons.
Refereeing and running the line.
Supporting Lincoln City for...........
a very long time.
Working for the matchday catering.
Running the London marathon to raise funds towards the new St Andrew Stand.
Editing and producing
'The Yellowbelly' fanzine.
Driving a mini-van of mates to away games.
Becoming vice-chair of Lincoln City Membership Scheme.
Becoming chair of Lincoln City Supporters Trust
Being elected to the board of directors as fans representative.
Summarising matches on local radio.
Becoming chairman of Lincoln City from 2000 to 2005
(for the second time - the first time lasted 16 hours).
Being assistant treasurer, PA announcer, and turnstile operator for Lincoln City Ladies FC.
Being Poacher the mascot at a Lincoln City Ladies game at Sincil Bank.
Being elected as a director of Supporters Direct.
Writing articles about, you've guessed it, football.

Rob is a firm believer in supporters playing a part in the running of their clubs. Donations from this book are intended to raise some modest funds for supporters trusts to help in their aims to do just that.

TO

Polly
Wills, Claire and Charlie
Matty and Mel
Robert, Heather, Holly and Stanley
Mum

and to the memory of
Keith Alexander

WRITING WRONGS

"Bugger," said Des as he slammed the phone down. Or, more accurately, as he made to slam it down to within a few inches of the receiver. The second thoughts he'd quickly had made him complete its descent more slowly as he put it back into position. His sports editor had rung about Town's game at Torquay tomorrow and casually advised him that, rather than make his own way on the long journey down to Devon, he'd arranged for Des to travel with Andy North, football commentator. Save on his mileage claim, his boss had said. And sentence Des, he believed, to hour after hour of tedious conversation when he'd looked forward to a solitary journey.

He slouched from the hall and slumped on to the settee. The TV was on, inevitably tuned in to the rolling satellite sports news channel, Des's staple diet. Jo sat quietly curled up on the other end of the settee, doing what she always did that time of the evening - reading. The presenter waffled on about another potentially mind-blowing transfer fee for another mind-blowingly average Premier League player, while the running news band along the bottom of the screen passed from cricket to women's cricket to the latest Premier League news.

Inevitably, as the latest League 2 news approached, the bit that mattered to Des, they broke for an ad break and the programme resumed in time for a rerun of the cricket, women's cricket, and Premier League information. The presenter introduced an 'exclusive' interview from the previous evening with a harassed Championship manager following a controversial defeat. On being asked for his views on the referee, he showed restraint by saying that there was no point in criticising him because it would do no good and he'd only end up in trouble with the FA again. He mentioned, in the midst of his statement about how he wasn't prepared to comment on the match officials, that he hoped the referee wouldn't be appointed to one of his games in the near future. The interviewer then asked, oblivious to the previous answer, if the team would hope they wouldn't be officiated by those officials again this season. Des leaned forward from his slumped position as the manager, more irritated then ever, showed even more restraint by saying, "well yes, as I've just mentioned, that wouldn't be great."
"You useless pillock, he's just said that," said Des, and, turning to Jo whilst pointing to the TV, asked, "Did you hear that? How do they get those jobs? Bloody how?"
"Who knows," she said, without averting her eyes from her book. Then, looking at Des, she asked "You know your parents are coming on Sunday?"

"Er, yeah, afternoon I hope."
"For lunch, and the afternoon - you'll be back in time?"
"Should be."

Des and Jo always enjoyed his parents' visits. Her mum and dad lived close by, but his lived the other side of the country and, ironically, since his father's retirement, their visits were less frequent. Just as he had lived his working life putting in long hours, Desmond senior spent his retirement doing the range of activities he'd always planned to do and he was as busy as ever. Father and son had always been close, which included enjoying a mutual passion during Des's youth for their local non-league club. The only area that Des's dad could never reconcile himself to was his son's choice of career. Desmond believed that journalism was far from an honourable profession. He had spent over forty years running an engineering company where things to him were straightforward and precise; he'd wished his son had chosen to work with him. Instead, he believed Des had entered an industry where being cunning was an important characteristic in succeeding - and possessing a lack of integrity wasn't necessarily a drawback. Des could always see his father's point of view, even if he didn't agree with it. It was the blandness of his present job and the refusal of his paper, just like any local rag anywhere, to allow him to write the things that he wanted to write that he found the most frustrating thing at this stage of his career. His paper was one of the club sponsors and the club relied on ticket offers publicised by it for extra income. The editor and the club chairman were good friends and both of their businesses enjoyed a cosy mutual back-scratching relationship.

Des would console himself that these must be only temporary worries. He had belief in his ability and was equally confident that he would sooner, rather than later, get a position with one of the better nationals. Once there, he would investigate the areas he was concerned with and write the way he wanted to, unhindered by editorial policy or his paper's incestuous relationship with the subject.

• • •

Like a lot of things that your first reaction says will be awful but then don't turn out as bad, the journey the next morning was surprisingly pleasant. Andy, Des reminded himself, was a decent bloke. Having been at the radio station for far too long without moving onward and upward he'd also become an avid Town fan. Without doubt, his radio shows were dreadful and his commentaries weren't much better, but Des admired Andy's passion for the club. He also hosted a Friday evening preview show and Des guested on it from time to time, if someone from either the club or the supporters' trust wasn't available. At times, when Andy first started at the station, he would get into a terrible muddle with these shows. Due to the usual financial constraints, presenters were expected to present and produce at the same time and, because of a lack of technical ability, Andy had occasionally ended up broadcasting either dead air or long periods of muzak while he anxiously tried to solve the problems he'd caused and resume his football chatter.

Inevitably, a lot of their conversation centred on the club including the team's performances, the players, the board, the staff and, most of all, the manager Paul Johnson. Andy loved the club, so he saw no bad in anyone, least of all the manager. Des, on the other hand, thought he was a complete arse. For professional reasons he never revealed this view.

Johnson the player had been an uncompromising centre-half and was a one-club man. He captained his team in the last three years of his playing career and his finest moment came in his last-but-one season when he led them to play-off victory at Wembley and promotion to League 1. His step up to management had not been as smooth and Town were his fourth club as a coach or manager. Many people felt that if he did not do well at Town this season he would have to go and would struggle to find another job - in the Football League anyway.

Des thought Johnson was a bully. He thought he had his favourites in the squad and his team was picked on the basis of whether he liked a player as a person or not. He was arrogant and ran rings around his chairman, who showed a complete inability to manage the manager. Because Johnson sensed these views, he tolerated Des at best. More often than not, Des would question the manager when others were around. After games, he would fire questions at him with other reporters and the local radio guys alongside. On a Thursday morning however, Des met Johnson at the ground in his office for an interview alone prior to the coming Saturday's fixture; whilst the common good meant their exchanges were civilised, their dislike for each other bubbled under the surface. Des always took work with him to the ground when he went to these meetings because Johnson always kept him waiting and he would have to sit in the car killing time. The interviews would often be interrupted by Johnson's mobile phone. He would answer and then carry on a conversation, even if it was only a fellow manager or a mate who rang for a chat. Johnson answered Des's questions abruptly but, when he could see Des was becoming irritated, he would become more helpful until he felt he could test his interviewer once again.

As they approached Torquay, Andy and Des agreed to meet up later after the game. They were both staying overnight and, because Torquay was a favourite away trip for a lot of Town fans, they knew a fair few would be out at night. Andy told Des that one of his college pals worked for a station in Devon and he would be meeting him during the evening. He also said that some of the girls from the club office were travelling down for the game and were making a weekend of it. On hearing this last bit of information, Des's enthusiasm for the day and night ahead grew markedly.

The match was unremarkable. Town held out for a 0-0 draw so, for the faithful 200 or so away fans, the point gained made it worthwhile but, to Des, the display was typical of the season so far. The team had little shape and the home keeper wasn't called on to make a single meaningful save. Johnson's team played what he had earlier described as an attacking formation, but the three strikers he'd said would cause Torquay problems actually comprised two wide midfielders, who kept dropping back to help in midfield, and Baines, who lacked pace and hardly had a touch up front.

As with any Johnson team, the defence looked sound but had they conceded, Des couldn't see any way that Town would have got back into the game. He watched the manager during the match and he performed his usual repertoire of arm-waving, harassing the fourth official, and turning to give humorous replies to the home fans' taunts. The players just about remembered to applaud the away fans at the final whistle, but it turned out the point didn't prevent Town from dropping a place in the table to sixteenth. Even though it was only September, promotion, or even the play-offs, seemed a long way off.

Des quickly emailed a brief match report back to base for the paper's website. Like a lot of local papers, they had stopped printing a Saturday evening 'Green Un' which had saddened the more ardent fans. They treated it as a ritual, waiting at the newsagents just before closing time, for them to arrive bundled up and tied with string. Sadly, not enough were sold to keep this viable. The immediacy of the website had contributed to its demise too. Tomorrow Des would write a longer, more reflective, report ready for Monday's edition of the paper.

He then waited in the corridor below the main stand for the manager to appear from the away dressing room and take questions from reporters and local radio people. Des enjoyed this because the manager was often more unguarded than when he was interviewed in calmer situations. As usual, Andy did a live interview which took place just before his station's sport show drew to a close; Des smiled at Andy's enthusiastic but banal questions.

Johnson said how he thought it was a good point and how the lack of quality in the final ball was the reason they didn't nick a goal. He said he was pleased with his team's defending and if they could string an unbeaten run together there was no reason they still couldn't get into the promotion places or a play-off spot. There was still a long way to go he said, and so on.

Andy thanked Johnson and then, when he heard that he was off air, thanked him profusely again. The manager then moved over to take questions from the press reporters there, one of them a girl from the Torquay equivalent of Des's paper. As expected, Johnson was dismissive and patronising with her and answered a couple of her questions with another question.

"Are you happy with the point?" she asked.

"I'd sooner have had all three, sweetheart. What do you think?"

"Did you think Torquay played the better football on the day?"

"No - did you?" he replied smiling.

Des was irritated by the way he dealt with her, but he had a job to do, so questioned him about the pattern of the game, the injury to Bleasdale, the decision to replace regular keeper Brown with loanee Henderson, and the Torquay goal that was ruled out for offside. Des really wanted to say that he thought the lack of invention in the team, and the lack of any single threatening attack on the home side's goal, made him wonder if he had any idea what he was doing. He knew that this would not be an advisable approach to take for a huge variety of reasons. Because the team hadn't lost, the interview was generally good-natured and Johnson stayed with them for a reasonable time before Ron the kit man poked his head round the corner and said that the team coach was ready to leave.

Ever helpful, Andy gave Des a lift to his guest house in town and they agreed to meet up in the same pub as they had last season, in an hour or so. Des had stayed at The Hollies before and Eric and Maureen greeted Des like a long-lost friend as he entered the hallway. In his room, Des rang Jo and they mutually questioned each other about how they were, what they'd done and what the weather was like there. Jo told him how she'd been working on her thesis all day and that she'd probably go and see her sister and the new baby in the morning. Just as he was about to say his farewells, Jo asked him to hang on because she'd just remembered he'd got what could an interesting letter in the post that morning.

"It's from the Mail - do you want me to get it?" she asked.

"What! Of course I do, bloody hell!"

He imagined Jo had got the phone cramped between the side of her chin and her shoulder as she opened the envelope and he heard the sound effects of paper tearing and being unfolded.

"It's from the sports editor, er Polish name, er do you pronounce it..."

"...doesn't matter how you pronounce it - what does it SAY?!" he interrupted.

"OK, no need to get stroppy – 'thank you for your blah blah'," she summarised, " 'would like you to attend for an interview...' ."
"Get in!!" Des said, "sorry for being arsey, that's fantastic - when is it?"
"Next Thursday, in their Manchester office."
"There is a god! Thank you, sweetheart. That's fantastic. Love you."
"Cupboard love," she said. "Well done, anyway. I know you've been desperate to hear from them."
They said their farewells and, as Des put the phone down, he felt elated.

• • •

Maureen made Des a sandwich and sat with him in the residents' lounge, telling him about how things at the guest house had been going that summer. She said she thought there had been an upturn in trade since the recession because fewer people were going abroad and Torquay getting back into the Football League had helped a bit too. She asked about Jo, who had come with Des when the two teams met last time, and Des confirmed that they hoped to start a family before long.

After a quick wash and brush up, Des walked down to the seafront to meet Andy and, on the way, thought about his forthcoming interview. He'd applied for two jobs with the big guys in the last six months and they'd come to nothing. In all honesty, he couldn't stand the Mail, who were owned by the same parent company as his own provincial paper - but he was prepared to shelve that view along with his political principles if it meant he could work at a higher level, doing the job the way he wanted. Having the ambition of working further up the ladder was his way of coping with the restrictions of his present job. And, on days when he was fully in daydreaming mode, he wished Jo and he could move somewhere isolated and he could write all day about the things he chose.

He recalled his early years with the Bugle and how the work was not what he expected. He spent hour after hour, week after week, in the local courts watching sad, lonely people, heads bowed, quietly weeping; defiant young men winking to their mates in the public gallery; and menopausal women who'd shoplifted without knowing it. Two weeks into the job he was told to follow up a poll tax story where a two-week-old baby had received a tax demand from the local council. He remembered walking up the garden path between two rusty bicycles and an old fridge lying in the long grass to be met at the front door by a tattooed guy in a vest holding said baby. He showed Des the poll tax bill with him, his partner, and young Brittany all listed as liable for the debt. Back at the office Des rang the revenues department at the council offices who said they didn't normally comment on such cases but they could confirm that they'd received a tax form with all three people listed as over eighteen. So despite the council not being at fault and the half-wit he'd met earlier having filled in the form wrongly, he was told to write a shock-horror 'baby-billed-for-poll-tax' story. This was an early hint at what a local journalist had to put up with.

Andy was already at the bar when Des walked in. Andy said he was in the chair and Des had already decided he was going to have a few beers over the next few hours to celebrate the interview, even if he couldn't reveal the good news. In the last few months, Des had curbed his drinking a lot because it was getting a bit out of hand. At least according to Jo it was.

Already there were a few Town fans wandering about and Fat Bloke, as he was affectionately known, walked into the pub with a couple of mates. They stood near Des and Andy. As soon as he saw his local media guys, he joined them. Des, to his shame, didn't know Fat Bloke's proper name, even though he'd spoken to him many times. To be fair, not many people knew his name and he was more than happy to be known by his less-than-flattering nickname, something he encouraged by having 'Fat Bloke' emblazoned on the back of his replica Town shirt. What Des did remember was that he always paused before he spoke, so having a conversation with him was like speaking on the phone to someone in Australia. If you asked him a question, there was a brief time delay before you got an answer and, if you weren't patient and allowed for this, you'd speak and then speak again at the same time as he got round to replying to your first comment. A three-way conversation, or more, became even more complicated.

Fat Bloke had started drinking as soon as the match had ended and he launched into a tirade about Town's performance, how 'shit the players were', how the striker 'couldn't hit a cow's arse with a banjo', how the manager hadn't got a clue, and finally how the board weren't ambitious enough and didn't want the club to get promoted. Andy and Des nodded politely and smiled weakly and Des hoped, even more than he did already, that things would go well on Thursday. Andy asked Fat Bloke if he was travelling back that night or in the morning and, forgetting his slow response time, asked him again just as he started to reply. Des decided he needed a second drink.

As time passed, the pub became busier with quite a few locals and a few more Town fans wandering in. Jack, the chair of Town's supporters trust and Hayley, the trust's representative on the club board, walked in together deep in conversation. Hayley had been elected by the fans earlier that year and this was her first season as a director. She was a pleasant middle-aged woman and, as well as being a keen fan, she was an ardent advocate of the trust movement. She often visited trusts at other clubs to advise them and speak about her experiences at her home town club. Probably because Jack was well-meaning but could talk for Britain, she waved across the room to Des and, putting her hand up to Jack and then pointing to Des in a gesture that said "hang on, I'm just going over there", she walked over to him smiling.
"Had a good day?" Des asked.
"Oh you know," she replied "An away point gained, I suppose, but the natives are getting restless."
"Are you getting it in the neck?"
"Goes with the territory I'm afraid. I'm the go-between between the board and the fans, but when the results are dodgy and we're well down the league I get a fair bit of stick."
"What are they saying?" asked Des.
"They're supportive of most things about the club but the manager rubs them up the wrong way. They want to know what the board think about him, but I can't reveal things like that."

At that moment, the door opened and four women entered. Three of them worked in the reception-cum-ticket office at Town's ground and one in the club shop. The last of them to walk in was Rosie, who immediately saw Des and smiled. Town were probably like any other football club when it came to working relationships, private relationships, gossip, and affairs. The women who worked there did so surrounded by testosterone-fuelled jack-the-lad footballers and one or two of them had a name, very probably unfairly, for having had relationships, brief or otherwise, with some of the players or backroom staff. One woman, an older one, was rumoured to have slept with over half the youth team.

Right from day one, as the local football reporter, Des had been attracted to Rosie. She was fresh-faced, friendly, intelligent and, most of all, exuded an air of innocence - something that made her stand out from the others. She had a boyfriend and, of course, Des had Jo, but they instantly got on. While Des was happy that this was a platonic friendship, he couldn't resist wondering what it would be like if Rosie was 'his' and how nice it would be, in a romantic way, to sleep with her. As usual, Des felt guilty about these thoughts and he reminded himself he could never cheat on Jo. He reassured himself by recalling some advice a mate at college had given him when he said that "there's now't wrong with a bit of window shopping, mate."

Des continued his conversation with Hayley and, as Rosie and friends walked past, he said "You OK? I'll come over for a chat in a bit." She smiled and nodded, while she continued her conversation with her friend alongside.

Andy came over carrying two pints and gave one to Des. Hayley carried on talking about the club, but Des was becoming bored with her. Whilst she was the fans' representative in the boardroom, the last person she was going to reveal a bit of interesting information to was the reporter from the local rag. She was being as wary as ever about letting something confidential slip out. Jack then launched into a long description of all the fundraising events the trust were planning in the coming months, clearly in the hope Des would give them some free publicity. Des would have normally taken all this in because, even socially, this was part of his job, but tonight he was in a good mood and he wanted to have a decent time.

Rosie and friends made to leave and Des was pleased that she told him they'd be 'over the road' when they brushed past. A couple of locals who had been to the game had come over to talk to the Town contingent, and Andy's mate arrived. He was Devon's answer to Alan Partridge, but by now the alcohol was kicking in and Des was in high spirits. Then Town's assistant manager, Danny Ford, walked in with a couple of guys. They'd put a bit of sponsor money into the club and enjoyed being hangers-on to some of the players or back-room staff in return. Des asked Danny why he was there and not on the team coach, and Danny said he'd got friends in the area from his time playing for Torquay many years ago and was staying with them for the weekend. Des liked Danny because he wasn't afraid to speak his mind and he often stood up for the players when Johnson had publicly criticised them. Des often thought Danny would be a good manager for Town because he knew his stuff. He suspected a lot of his ideas for the squad in terms of tactics and the type of players to bring in were quashed by his boss because Johnson's ego wouldn't allow them.

Fat Bloke was nearby and he was in full voice. When Danny and Des heard the words 'sometimes wonder if he's been to the same fucking game' they both laughed, knowing it was a comment on Des's reporting skills.
"What pearls have you come up with for today's performance then, Des, old son?" asked Danny.
"Oh you know, hard-earned point, tight affair, stuff like that."
"Fair enough mate but picking the wrong team didn't help. Don't bloody quote me mind; we're off duty," said Danny.
Des by now was semi-drunk and he couldn't resist following this comment up.
"You don't rate Johnson much do you, Danny?"
"He's my boss and my friend - I just think he's losing it sometimes. By the way, he fucking hates you."
"What? I only do my job," said Des,
"You're clever and you know about football. He doesn't like that," said Danny.

"Yeah well, I reckon he's not as good as he fucking thinks he is," and, with that, Des went off in search of another drink.

• • •

Des woke up with his head pounding. He crawled out of bed, went into the bathroom, and was sick in the toilet. His head was swimming, not only with a pounding headache, but with confusion about the last couple of hours of the night before. His thoughts, although muddled, centred on the job interview, on hearing that the manager was slagging him off, his response about that to his assistant, and the vague memory he had of trying it on with Rosie in the wine bar late on in the evening. He felt ill, elated, angry, and anxious all rolled into one. Just then his mobile rang. It was Andy.
"Here, mate; ready for off."
"What?"
"Half-eight mate. Said I'd pick you up at half-eight."
"OK," said Des. "Get 'em to make you a coffee and I'll be down in a minute."
When he answered Andy's call Des noticed he'd had a text, timed at around midnight. "enjoyed ur company c u soon R xxx," it said. The anxiety bit of his hangover subsided.

Des showered, threw his stuff in his holdall, tidied the bed man-style, and went downstairs. Andy sat reading a Sunday paper, looking refreshed and ready for the trek home but then, sensible as ever, he'd turned in early last night and hadn't carried on drinking like his travelling companion. Des gulped a black coffee, paid Eric and thanked him. The guest house, as usual, exuded calm and comfort and it seemed wrong to dash off so quickly, especially in front of his hosts who were the sort of people to whom slow was the only pace. However, Des didn't want to put out Andy any more than he had already and, more importantly, he had his parents' visit to get back for.

Because it was Sunday morning, the roads were clear and, for all his faults, thought Des, at least Andy had a tendency to put his foot down and they made good progress. Andy tried to make conversation but Des feigned nodding off, so instead he resorted to randomly searching the local BBC and commercial channels listening to his counterparts' efforts. Eyes closed, but awake, Des thought about things that had happened over the weekend. He was angry that Johnson had criticised him because he wanted people who he dealt with to see that he was professional at what he did, whatever the constraints he worked under. That was what made him angry, not because it was a cheap personal insult. At the same time, Des felt guilty that he'd opened up in return in front of Danny because he knew what he'd said would go straight back to Johnson; and the working relationship, if there ever was one, would be even more tenuous.

He thought about Rosie and imagined, because of the text, that he hadn't messed up. From its tone, if you can assess a tone from a text, he thought he may even have made progress. Then, as usual, he metaphorically pinched himself telling himself that even though he thought she was wonderful and she clearly (maybe) liked him, he had Jo and he needed to buck up and stop acting like a love-sick kid. He also imagined that those very honourable statements of loyalty had been expressed by around a million billion blokes in his position in the past, and a zillion others would unconvincingly say the same in the future. With inevitable results.

• • •

Jo drove, with Des alongside her and his parents in the back of her car. It was his parents' wedding anniversary and they were going for a late lunch to celebrate in a bistro that Jo liked in a modern retail and leisure development on the edge of town. Having recovered from the hangover, but still tired from the journey and the weekend generally, Des recalled how he had been there once before when he interviewed Henderson, the new keeper Town had recruited on loan from Huddersfield. Just as he did the first time, Des marvelled at the buildings with their steep roofs and central tower over an arched entrance as they came into view from the new tree-lined approach road. He wondered about the architects who spent months (maybe years) on its design, who then revised it all when the developer had his say and the planners had their way. And at the end of this process of interference, compromise, and cost-cutting they ended up with a building that looked for all the world, thought Des, like fucking Auschwitz. He thought architecture must be an absurd profession. Just like his own.

In the restaurant, they ordered food and drink, and Jo gave her in-laws a present and a card. Des smiled knowingly and modestly when they opened the present, whilst not having a clue what it was, because Jo had bought it the day before. They discussed all the expected subjects and shared any news they had to offer. Des's mum told them about everything his dad had been up to, which reminded Des of the three constants in their lives: the indefatigable quest Desmond had to live his life usefully, how his mum lived her life through her husband, and her role to always tell people about his activities. The last was something he would never do through modesty and the belief that everything he did was important to him but must surely be insignificant to anyone else. She told Des and Jo how he had been asked by a friend to do some lecturing to mechanical engineering students, and he was preparing his syllabus notes for that. She said he still went jogging, and last week he'd fitted a replacement boiler in the kitchen. Des felt he needed to tell them about his forthcoming interview and what the job entailed. Knowing that his father would not want to disappoint him with his reaction, but would probably show only token interest, he revealed that if he got the job his role would not involve reporting on matches but would be more investigative. He would have the freedom to look into issues concerning things like club finances, agents, transfers - in short the real events on and off the pitch. He would be able to write with freedom and he would feel he was doing the job the way he always wanted to. Des then realised that he'd been describing the new position for over twenty minutes. He also realised that all the way through it, his father had been looking across the table at him listening attentively, and nodding and smiling - he dared to believe - approvingly. As Des finished, Desmond senior asked, "Does that mean you won't ever have to say again that the manager is going to take one game at a time?"
Out of the blue, Des replied, almost involuntarily, "I love you, dad."

And whilst his mum, dad and Jo were taken aback by this show of emotion (so much so that it made Jo cough, forcing a trickle of gravy to run down from the corner of her mouth), they all realised it had been an aptly honest moment.

• • •

Des's match report and associated interviews were in Monday's edition and on the website. He monitored the website where fans could post their comments. These fell roughly into two camps - the realists and the pessimists. Optimists were hard to find since the season started. Supporters' views on the board, the manager, the squad, the style of play and the league position were, at best, in the 'what do you expect' camp, bearing in mind Town's history of existing mainly in the bottom division; and, at worst, in the 'it's all shit - we're doomed' school of thought. Contributions were often basic and blunt whilst others, Des felt, showed imagination and humour. Hardly any actually bore the writer's name and often ended with a nom-de-keyboard which probably meant that only their mates knew who they were. A point away from home was generally acceptable, whatever league position Town were in, but an undercurrent of impatience was there for all to see.

On Tuesday Des rang Danny Ford. He wouldn't have been doing his job if he hadn't followed up their chat on Saturday night when Danny let his guard slip. It would also give Des the opportunity to smooth over the observations he'd made about Danny's boss.
"Hi mate. It's Des."
"Who?"
"Des, from the paper."
"Oh yeah, sorry mate. Was miles away," said Danny.
"How's it going? Just thought I'd give you a ring after our chat. How's Paul?"
"OK mate - both OK – look, can I ring you back, something's kicked off here and I've got to sort it out."
"Yes of course, I'll ring you… ."
Des heard Danny's mobile go dead.

From Danny's tone and the background noise, Des thought this was probably more than the normal behind-the-scenes training chaos, but it was hard to tell if it was anything significant.

Next morning, as arranged, Des interviewed club captain Sean Gibbs. This was another challenge because Sean may have been the leader on the pitch, but he certainly wasn't a straight talker or free thinker when it came to interviews off it. On the rare occasion he was interviewed on local television, he failed to realise that the interviewer wanted more than one- or two-word answers and a cheeky smile. He was, however, a thoroughly pleasant bloke and liked a chat off the record. It was just that he hadn't bridged the gap between his private manner and his official role. They met at a leisure club on the edge of town and sat in the café looking over the pool. The difficulty with this interview, or rather the almost impossible task with this interview, was to glean something that didn't consign the article into the realm of the banal. There was no up-and-coming third round FA Cup tie against Premier League opposition to discuss, neither was there the arrival of a new manager to talk about. The interviewee was neither recently bought or was to be imminently sold. He hadn't led them to an impressive unbeaten run or hadn't scored in a series of consecutive matches. So unless Des found some gem to highlight this quiet midweek match-free period, he ran the risk of a reader posting something like 'captain says blah blah blah in pointless article shock', or some other mickey-taking contribution to the comments section. Sean said that the squad needed to play well for ninety minutes and not just small phases in each game, and they needed to string a run together. Gem-free so far. He said he felt he was playing OK and they were all doing the simple things well enough; they just needed a bit of luck or a bit of inspiration to start a good run going. And again. The dilemma of not wanting to drop Sean in it, but needing to find something interesting, led Des to tell him about his curtailed call with Danny, when he sensed something was wrong. Sadly Sean, after asking when that was, and confirming it would have been just before a training session, then brushed it off. He seemed slightly less comfortable than when he had been answering the earlier questions. Des carried on with the interview, deciding that he would highlight Sean's eager anticipation at playing his old club Barnet this coming

Saturday as the thrust of his article, and hope the public wouldn't be too hard on him or his subject.

When Sean had gone, Des bought another coffee and rang Barnet's manager. He asked him about Sean's time there for tomorrow's piece, and quizzed him about his team for Saturday for his Friday preview. He quickly knew he would have to resist the quote that 'Gibbs was a fucking useless captain', but would use the more complimentary comments about him playing through injuries and always giving one hundred per cent.

• • •

Des and Jo got up early on Thursday morning, and she waved him off as he drove down the road. He'd allowed himself masses of time and he was determined not to get delayed by traffic jams or anything else that would deter him from being in a good frame of mind for the interview. He didn't know how many were in for the job, but a few miles into the journey he decided one thing. He'd been to interviews before and said the things he thought they'd expected to hear. This time he was going to tell them what he wanted to say. If they wanted a journalist with a free reign they needed to know they'd got the right person, and no amount of pretence was going to tell them that. It was going to be an honest appraisal of what he would research and how he would write. No holds barred in the interview and no holds barred when he did the job. Des had got a bit of a name in the industry for campaigning for those who deserved it, but the conduit for this was never through his present employers. He'd had articles published elsewhere about clubs trading insolvently, club staff who'd lost their jobs while players received bonuses, and agents who'd acted for themselves first and their clients second. But he wanted to investigate the FA and reveal if it was as dysfunctional as he thought it was. Owners who bought clubs and loaded the cost back on to them so that, in effect, they bought themselves, should be exposed so that their fans revolted against it. He wanted to announce over the rooftops that the Premier League should be stopped from devouring the national game. Bodies such as the Football Supporters Federation and Supporters Direct asked him to speak at their conferences. But this was peripheral stuff. He wanted to do it full time. He loved the football industry and he hated it at the same time and he dearly wanted to use his skills to make a contribution towards putting it right. With the best will in the world, covering the fortunes of a small league club was boring and, he suspected, the way he had to do it was pretty damn boring to his readers too.

He arrived in good time, and was shown to a reception area where he waited patiently to be called. He tried to appear cool but was churning inside. There didn't seem to be any other candidates around but he felt on show to members of staff who walked past. Des consoled himself with the thought that waiting was the worst part, and he knew he had the confidence to project himself well when the real action started. After ten minutes, he was ushered into a small conference room, where around six people sat waiting for him. He hardly took in the names and positions of the editors, human resources, and finance people who introduced themselves to him. After some pleasantries, he was asked about how he would carry out the role were it offered to him. Then he was asked a series of ethical questions to establish how he would deal with delicate issues and avoid the paper facing repercussions. He tried to display professionalism but show them he was passionate about his subjects. They asked him some logistical questions, including where would he like to be based. He was delighted when they confirmed he could work from home and would probably only have to come to Manchester twice a week. He felt encouraged by this and was tempted to think they wouldn't have said this if he wasn't in with a chance of getting the job. After a period of time that seemed to fly by, but actually lasted well over an hour, they thanked him and stood up so that he could shake their hands.

Douglas, the MD, told him as he left that he would hear from them, and added:
"By the way, I think I know your father. Is he well?"
"Yes thanks, he's fine. How do you know him, if you don't mind me asking?"
"I started in engineering - he was my first boss. You've got the same name and your CV says where you used to live. Anyway, give him my regards and, as I've said, we'll be in touch."

As Des left the building and sat in his car for a few moments thinking maybe he'd done OK. He had good feelings about the place, the people there, and what they would expect of him if he was successful. He decided he'd have a steady drive home, sit and tell Jo all about it, and ring his dad to tell him too.

• • •

"Well, here we all are - eagerly anticipating another epic battle!"
So said Joe, the Barnet reporter, as he climbed the steps into the press box. He squeezed into a seat next to Des and they shook hands as best they could in the cramped surroundings. The two men asked after their respective wives, and talked about their clubs. There was a certain camaraderie amongst the local media people. Whilst the teams they followed would soon be battling for three points, Des, Andy and their counterparts wouldn't really be in competition. They often helped each other out when a scorer couldn't easily be identified or a player was involved in an off-the-ball incident. They all had clipboards, match programmes and stop watches and they were keen to get hold of a team sheet as soon as they could. Then they could assess the formations and form their opinions about players who were selected or left out.
"Your lads are in need of a win, old son," said Joe.
"Yeah, but it's early days," replied Des.
"Don't you believe it. Once you get stuck in the bottom two, it ain't easy to get out. And your lads are favourites for the drop I reckon, based on what I've seen so far."

The club secretary and Rosie walked up the steps each carrying team sheets for distribution to the media, before taking them into the executive club and boardroom. As Rosie passed by, Des surprised himself - and Joe - by asking her if she would be anywhere near the press room at half-time and, if so, if she'd have a coffee with him. She smiled and said she'd try her best.

All conversation ceased for a couple of minutes as the starting elevens were digested.
"He's dropped Marvin," said Pete, former Town player and Andy's summariser.

26

"Bloody hell," said Des, "what's going on?"

Marvin Tyler was probably the first name anyone connected with Town would pick for the first team. He had played for Jamaica and in his three years with Town had become a firm favourite. He was a speedy winger who could get behind defences, but he knew what was needed in this division and had quickly learned to track back and defend when it was needed. He wasn't on the bench either so Des assumed he was injured or ill, although no-one around him could confirm so.

In front of a poor crowd of around three-and-a-half thousand, Sean Gibbs led the players out. Town attacked the home end in the first half. As usual they had most of the early possession but Barnet looked the most likely to create a chance. They had two small stocky guys in midfield and, after the first twenty minutes, they started to run the show. The Town fans got more and more restless and when Baines headed six feet over the bar from their only chance in the fortieth minute the fans behind the goal started a 'you don't know what you're doing' chant in the direction of the home dugout. It got worse just at the very moment the fourth official held up the sign to indicate a minute's added time when a long range shot rebounded off Henderson's chest and Barnet's teenage striker scrambled the ball home. During the break, Des looked around for Rosie, and she came in the press room just as he was leaving. She apologised for missing him, explaining that she'd had to spend a lot of time appeasing an unhappy sponsor. In the second half, Town tried to raise their game, and Gibbs tried to lift his team-mates but, apart from a shot that was cleared off the line, the equaliser never looked like coming. Des watched Johnson and compared him to the Barnet manager. Johnson berated the assistant referee near him and he did the same to the fourth official. He ranted and kicked the side of the dugout. His opposite number stood calmly with his arms folded taking in the action and assessing each situation. Before the game, general opinion would have it that, of the two managers, Barnet's young boss was the one who looked likely to progress up the leagues, with or without his present club. Today's displays confirmed it. The game petered out without further incident and the home players left the pitch to boos from the few fans who hadn't already left the ground.

Des emailed his report and, under the stand, Johnson eventually appeared from the dressing room, too late for a live interview on Andy's football show. He gave short sharp answers to the questions put to him and it was clear he was only tolerating the interviews because he was instructed to do them. He'd been fined by the board for missing them in the past. On being told Town were now only two points above the relegation places, he shrugged his shoulders. Des asked him why Tyler didn't play and Johnson spat out the reply ''cos he fucking didn't.' With that he muttered 'fucking arse' under his breath, turned, and went back down the corridor to his office.

After retrieving his stuff from the press box, Des, still angry from the reply he'd got from Johnson, went up the stairs, into the executive lounge and made for the stairs in the far corner. Sponsors and guests as well executive club members were in there drowning their sorrows, talking about the state of the club, and saying what they thought needed doing. In Des's experience, the people in this part of the ground were never short of an opinion on what the club needed to do.

A guy pulled at Des's arm as he walked past. "You got a minute?"
He was holding a glass of red wine and looked like he'd had a few already. "You're that bloke from the paper aren't you?"
"Afraid so."
"You know what's happened to Marvin don't you? He's had a scrap. Had that tosser Baines winding him up. Calling him 'names'. You know what I mean. Well, poor old Marvin decided he'd had enough and he gave the dickhead a good panning in the car park. Threw him over Fordy's car - his head dented the bonnet. "Course, Baines has got a thick skull but that prat of a manager drops Marvin, not the knobhead who started it. So we don't play our best player and we get beat. Put that in your fucking paper."
With that, he turned to a group of middle-aged men in suits and resumed his conversation with them.

● ● ●

Next morning, Des and Jo got up and made tea and toast. They scanned the Sunday papers - Jo starting from the front and Des from the back; their habits of a lifetime. Des would be preparing his Monday article that morning but recent events needed to be followed up first, even though his report would have to be about the game only. Sitting there in his boxers, he rang a few people to check on the rumour he'd heard after the game. Andy didn't know anything and probably wouldn't have said anything if he did. There was no reply from Danny's mobile but it was clear this was too serious an issue, if true, for an assistant manager to talk about behind his boss's back, so it was no great loss that he couldn't speak to him. A couple of other contacts didn't know about any fight between players. As a last resort, he rang Hayley. Expecting nothing, he was surprised by her response.

"This is off the record, right? I'm trusting you to keep this under your hat, but things are going from bad to worse with Johnson. Yes, there was a fight."

"Can you tell me more, Hayley?"

"Yes, I can and will," she said. "The players had a night out in town and Baines was out of order. He made racist jokes to Tyler in a night club and he carried on with them at the ground the next day. Marvin's as soft as anything but he'd had enough and confronted him. Baines took a swing at him and Marvin gave him a good hiding. Johnson sided with Baines and punished the wrong guy. It's sickened me, Des, that's why I'm telling you all this."

Des told her he sympathised because he knew the board would have to deal with it, and he knew the chairman would, as usual, back down when it came to dealing with the manager's behaviour. Tomorrow Des would be meeting Johnson at the club. Town had a game at Chesterfield on Wednesday night so he needed a piece for Tuesday. He decided it was going to be a very interesting interview.

That night Des and Jo sat together on the settee, for once finding a film they both fancied watching. Or rather, Des tried watching it but kept thinking about Johnson bad-mouthing him, the state of the club, the team, their position in the league and, most of all, the fight between the players. He had never been as consumed by things at the club as he was now. Then the phone rang. Des answered it and was transformed straight away into alert mode. It was Douglas, from the Mail.

"Sorry to ring on a Sunday, Des, but there's no nine-to-five in our business as I'm sure you know, so I hope you don't mind."

"That's fine, no problem."

"I though you'd like to know, sooner rather than later. We'd like to offer you the job. Not 100% definite, but not far off. Just a few logistical matters and a few salary tweaks to sort out. I'm hoping you can come in and we'll tie up the loose ends."

"Yes, fantastic, I'll be there. Tomorrow morning?" said Des.

Douglas chuckled. "No, old chap, I thought Wednesday, about eleven o'clock if that's OK."

"Wednesday will be great," said Des, and they said their goodbyes.

Next morning, Des busied himself in the office. He checked out the coverage of Saturday's game in the papers and on Barnet's website. He rang Town's general office to say he'd be there at lunchtime to interview Johnson, asking them to pass on the message. He felt like a child on his last day at school before the summer holidays, but he knew at last he'd made the career breakthrough he'd always longed for. At the same time, he felt angered by recent events at the club. The knowledge that he would soon be moving on wasn't enough to relieve these feelings, and he was realising how much a part of his life this little lower league club had been. He sat through an editorial meeting as the sport team planned their week, and he thought about the questions he'd put to Johnson later.

Des arrived at the club and went into reception. He could see into the general office and it was deserted except for a young man on work experience, putting unsold programmes into boxes. Des assumed that other people were out at lunch. Rather than wait for someone to help him, he went back outside and walked around to the players' entrance. He thought that, for once, he wasn't going to be kept waiting by the manager. If he could keep his side of the bargain and be there on time, Johnson could damn well see him straight away and not mess him about. The door back into the stand was open and, down the dimly lit corridor, a couple of players were walking towards

the dressing room. They wore only shorts and flip-flops and, because Monday was a day off for the squad, Des knew they would have come in to have injuries treated. Other than that, it was pretty quiet for an area that comprised changing rooms, treatment rooms, officials' accommodation, boot rooms and a laundry - where more often than not, it was bedlam. Des walked towards the manager's office at the end of one of the corridors. Just as he was going to knock and enter, in the gloom he felt a firm grip on his wrist. As he looked round, Danny Ford gently pulled him away and slowly led him back down the corridor.
"Hold on a mo', old son, I wouldn't go in there just yet," he said. As he said it, Des saw him wink and smile broadly to Ron who was leaning on the boot room door nearby, and who smiled in return.
"I've got an interview with your gaffer," said Des, annoyed by what had happened.
"You'll get your interview pal, it's just not convenient right now. Wait there. I'm sure he won't be long," said Danny and, irritatingly to Des, he grinned in Ron's direction once more. Des leaned against the frame of the open dressing room and waited. Yet again, he'd arrived on time and, although the interview was going to take place on a Monday instead of a Thursday, it was a quiet day. He thought that Johnson could co-operate for once, especially when he was under fire and needed any good media coverage he could get. He checked his watch and rechecked some of the questions he'd scribbled on his notepad. Just then Johnson's door opened slowly and, although it was gloomy, Des could make out a woman slowly backing out, presumably saying parting words to the person inside. She turned and adjusted her skirt. As she walked along the corridor, not noticing Des who took a step back into the changing room, he saw her fasten the top buttons of her blouse. Then, as she walked into the light, he could see it was Rosie, who didn't see him as she walked slowly past to the outside door and stepped back into the daylight.

Des was stunned, and his legs felt like jelly. He felt like he'd been kicked in the stomach. That arrogant bastard, he thought; and that girl. He thought she was pleasant and innocent, and all the time she's been letting that obnoxious bastard fuck the arse off her. He'd had her on his desk with his staff outside knowing what was going on.

31

And he'd sure as hell be bragging and crowing about it to his thick laughing mates, who'd all suck up to him and tell him what a great bloke he was for doing it.

In a trance, Des walked up to Johnson's door and went straight in. Johnson was sitting back in his leather swivel chair looking out of the window, and he turned round and greeted him sarcastically,
"Hello Desmondo. Do come in."
"I'm in a rush," said Des, the only thing he could think of saying as he sat down, "so I'll get straight to it. What do you think of Town's league position now we're in danger of relegation?"
"Relegation? It's only September; I could get manager of the month next month. Then we'd all be talking about promotion. Bit harsh that, mate."
"And your new keeper. Picked in preference to last season's player of the season. Definitely at fault for their goal don't you think?"
"He's saved us a good few points since he came," replied the manager firmly, becoming irritated by the questions.
"Town haven't scored for over 200 minutes and a lot of people are saying we don't create enough chances. What do you say to them?"
"Look, judge the team and me by where we are at the end of the season, OK?"
"How's your relationship with the board - do you think you still have their backing?" asked Des.
"Of course I fucking do. It's early days. Jesus Christ."
"Why was Marvin dropped?"
"Because I pick the fucking team and he was playing like a twat." answered Johnson, his voice raised much further.
"Nothing to do with the fight with Baines then?" asked Des, in the same, outwardly dispassionate, voice.
"There's been no fucking fight and this interview is now over. Fuck off out of here."
"No fight started by Baines, no fight that led to your lacky's car being damaged, no fight that meant the best player was dropped....."
With that Johnson stood up and, grabbing Des, bundled him across the office and pushed him out the door. As Des tried to regain his composure, Johnson shouted at him.
"You can stand up for that useless black twat if you like. And write

your shit. But don't ever come near me again or I'll rip your head off and stick it up your fucking arse."

With that the manager's door slammed shut. Danny Ford was there and asked Des what was going on. Des ignored him and went out into the car park.

• • •

Back at his office, Des shut the door behind him, threw his notepad down on to the desk, and switched on his computer. Using a password he had been given for the rare occasions when he needed to publish copy direct on to the website unchecked by a superior, he wrote the following article:

JOHNSON IN RACIST SLUR

"In an amazing attack on fans' favourite Marvin Tyler, Town manager Paul Johnson today launched a racist tirade about the player - something that is sure to land him and the club in serious trouble. Johnson, in language that this paper cannot repeat, criticised the player and refused to back him as rumours of players' unrest and fights continue to circulate around the club and amongst fans.

Johnson also refused to accept responsibility for the plight the club now find themselves in and confirmed that the board and staff are fully behind him. This is despite, however, members of the board and backroom staff saying privately that they feel he is letting the club down with poor player recruitment, bizarre team selections, and a lack of tactical ability.

Town face Chesterfield on Wednesday in turmoil. Defeat could see them in the relegation zone for the first time and facing a long hard winter to survive in the Football League. Clearly, in the light of the offensive remarks made by Johnson and internal problems, that will surely fester and grow if not dealt with, the chairman and the board must act fast. Removing the manager is their only option."

Des then pushed the 'send' button, turned off the computer, and left the building, switching his phone off as he stepped on to the pavement. He walked down the street and stopped at a cash machine, drawing out fifty pounds. Then he entered the Nelson pub a few of blocks down from the Bugle's offices, and ordered a pint of lager and a double vodka.

Two hours later, Des unlocked the door and entered the flat. Jo was out, no doubt still at college. He retrieved his phone from his jacket pocket and, looking at it for a few seconds, switched it back on. As it sprung into life it indicated he'd had eighteen missed calls. He listened to the first voice message, which was from Andy.
"What the fuck's going on, Des?" Des smiled, because that was the first time he'd heard Andy swear. "Your boss has gone ballistic and Town's chairman has fallen out with him big style. Sponsorship deals called off, the lot. The board are all at the ground at an emergency meeting. All hell let loose. What the fuck have you…" and with that Des deleted the message.

He went into the kitchen and found a half-full bottle of wine in the fridge. He took it into the lounge and sat at the window watching the drizzle. Just then the phone in the hall rang and he ignored it. A minute later it rang again, and he walked through slowly and answered it.

It was Douglas from the Mail. What he had to say was brief and to the point. Des politely said goodbye and gently hung up. He then went in to the lounge and switched on the television. The twenty-four-hour sports news channel came on, and he turned it off. He sat down at the window again and watched as the rain got heavier.

MAN MANAGING

"If you don't take your hand off my knee, you'll get this jug of water over your bloody head."
"Sorry, Sally. I'm lonely. You know that."
"That's the fourth time you've tried that. I'm a friend - that's all. Just pull yourself together man. She only left you a month ago. You haven't had time to get lonely. Now pour me some more wine."

Sally and Reggie were in a little Italian restaurant in Newark's Market

Place. This was the third time she'd agreed to meet him since her husband and his wife had run off together. They hadn't had an inkling anything was going on but then, out of the blue, they both got texts saying their spouses had left to run a bar together in Majorca and they wouldn't be back. Sally was prepared to meet Reggie because he had taken it badly and she didn't mind helping. Unfortunately, in his confused state, he was clearly hoping the natural outcome of these events was that he and Sally would get together. She wasn't interested in that. Reggie might be shattered that Deirdre had left him, but Sally wasn't going to let Dave's departure get to her. She was going to fight back.

"Have you heard from Dave?" asked Reggie.
"No, and I don't want to" replied Sally." He hasn't even had the decency to contact Martin, his own son. He's a shit."
"Deirdre's stuff is all over the house. It's like the Marie Celeste. After all I did for her. She didn't want for anything. Life of bloody luxury. Holidays, cruises, health spas, golf club. The lot. She went shopping for clothes every day. I even think she was shagging the bloody gardener. I reckon they used to do it in the greenhouse, and I turned a blind eye to it. I did everything for that woman."
"Did everything my arse. You're a piss artist and you've been no bloody angel. You've tried getting off with me many a time. And you spend most of your time at that bloody football club," said Sally.
"Yeah, and look where it's got me. My bloody wife has gone off with my bloody manager. The bastards."

Reggie Grainger was owner and chairman of Newark United F.C. He had set them up from nothing and, in the space of six seasons, they had reached Blue Square North, just two steps below the Football League. They started out as tenants of the local rugby club and two years later bought them out. Reggie had developed the site and they now had a neat modern ground on the outskirts of town with a capacity of four and a half thousand. Two sides were covered, with a busy social club under one of the stands. The players were part time, but were on good money. His manager, the recently departed Dave Hampton, Sally's husband, was a full-time employee of the club. Reggie made his fortune supplying fancy goods, or 'crap' as Sally called it, to all the gift shops on the east coast, and money and the football club were his two obsessions.

Sally met Dave when he was a young player at Ipswich. Her father was manager there for twelve seasons, until he had to retire through ill health. She used to go to all the games and, back at home, dad and daughter used to talk football together for hours on end. Ipswich had some good years in that period, including a Carling Cup final appearance. As a teenager Sally steered clear of the players. Dave was persistent though, and she agreed to go out with him after he kept calling in at the bank where she worked. They got married after a long engagement and Martin, their son, now played in midfield for Newark. Dave had played lower league and non-league football for a range of clubs in the Midlands. After being first team coach at Kidderminster and then manager at Eastwood, he applied for, and got, the Newark job. Sally worked for a bank in the town and, although their marriage wasn't great, things were ticking over OK. Or so she thought.

"You need to gather up all her stuff and give it to charity. Then move house. Start again." said Sally.
"Will you help me Sal?" asked Reggie. "I can't do all that on my own."
"God, you're useless. How the hell you made all that money I'll never know. Soon as your appalling bloody wife leaves you, you fall apart. Dave's stuff went in a skip the day after I found out. I'm looking to the future, not moping. And I'm not taking any shit from anyone any more. I'm going to live for me from now on."
"You're right."
"And what about the club? You need a new manager. If you need reminding," asked Sally, as a waiter wandered near to their table.
"I've got Jez doing it for now. I can't get my head round getting a new bloke in. Not just yet."
"If that bloody waiter doesn't stop hovering round I'm going to give him what for," said Sally, annoyed. "Jez is a complete prat. The players don't respect him and his coaching methods are crap. Why Dave brought him in god only knows."
"I'll make some calls. There'll be plenty of people who'll want to

manage Newark. We're on the way up. Lots of potential. I'll get a good bloke, you'll see."

"Make sure you do. And Martin will enjoy not having his dad pick on him all the time," said Sally.

"You like-a some more vino?" asked the waiter, leaning over Sally.

"No," she replied.

"You like-a I......"

"Will you bugger off. You've been hovering round all bloody night getting on my wick. And you can pack in talking in that crappy Italian accent. You're called Melvyn. You're from Mansfield, not Milan. I've seen you pissed in the social club, gobbing off after a Newark home match. So piss-a off-a."

"Soz Mrs 'ampton," said Melvyn, as he slouched away.

"I see what you mean about not taking any more shit, Sal," said Reggie.

"Just watch me", said Sally.

• • •

Next morning, Sally arrived at the bank with a hangover and little enthusiasm for the day ahead. She had a brief chat with her boss Mr Wilks, before going through her emails and reading instructions from head office about yet more new banking practices. Sally was only forty-five but the way banks operated had changed drastically from her early years as a cashier in Ipswich. Mr Wilks was a nice enough chap, but he did nothing to stand up for his staff as the demands from head office became more and more onerous. Sally manned the enquiries desk and was in the front line when it came to placating angry customers. After recent events, she had decided enough was enough and she thought she might give up the banking ghost once and for all. The bank opened on time and a steady stream of customers came in. Most went up to the cashiers, but a queue formed at Sally's desk. She knew it was going to be a bad day when an agitated man came up to her.

"I've been using this bank for nearly twenty years," he said. "I've got a query on my savings account. Over there, they told me they couldn't deal with it. Said I had to use the customer service phone on the wall. I've picked it up, and it's a bloody call centre in India. So I come into my own bank in my own home town and I have to speak to someone in bloody Mumbai. Jesus bloody Christ."

"Yes," said Sally, "that's what they make you do. But give me the details and I'll sort it out for you." She then leaned over to him and whispered "You're right, it's rubbish. I should change banks if I was you."
"Thank god you're here," said the customer.
Then an old lady who'd waited patiently for fifteen minutes approached her.
"I'm Mrs Shaw. I'm eighty-six. I've cashed cheques here for years. That young lady says you don't do that any more. Said I've had warning, and they won't cash cheques under two hundred pounds. I only want twenty pounds. Get some cat food and an ironing board cover. I get my pension on Thursday."
"Bless you, Mrs Shaw. Yes, another new policy. It's to get you to use your card in the cash dispenser."
"But I don't know how…."
"It's OK," Sally interrupted, "just hold on."

She went into the back office and took out a twenty-pound note from a tin. It was the collection for Mr Wilks' sixtieth birthday present from the staff.
"The silly old bugger doesn't deserve a bloody present," Sally said to herself, and she handed the note to the lady.
"You take this as a present from the bank, Mrs Shaw. Just let's keep it our little secret." said Sally.
"Bless you dear." said Mrs Shaw, as she smiled and left the bank.

At lunch, Sally rested in the staff room with Denise, a colleague and good friend. They had lots of things in common, including liking football and hating the bank. Just then Sally's mobile phone rang. Her son Martin's name was displayed.
"Hi mum, how's it going?" he asked.
"Fine, absolutely fine." said Sally. She didn't pass on any of her worries to her son, believing he, too, had enough to contend with, his dad having gone off with another woman.

"Good. I'm ringing to let you know I'm working right through 'til training tonight, so I won't be home 'til later."
"OK, Martin. Ta for letting me know." she said.
"I was thinking about not bothering, 'cos the guy doing it is shit. But I want to stay in the team, so I'll have to."
"Is it that bad love? I'd heard it was poor."
"Grandad would turn in his grave if he knew what this Jez pillock gets us to do," said Martin.
"Well that's not on. I've a good mind to ring Reggie."
"No, don't do that. I don't want to grass him up, even if he is rubbish. We'll have a new boss soon anyway, I hope."
"Sooner rather than later, hey love. I might come and watch. Would you mind?" asked Sally.
"You used to when dad was here. Not a problem, see you later then."

Sally left work and went shopping at Tesco. Over the last few weeks, she'd realised how even the most mundane things were affected by a marriage break-up. Even shopping at a supermarket. It wasn't just the obvious effect, like buying less food, and not having to remember the ointment for her husband's piles. It was the whole thing. She was a single person and the place was full of couples. And she didn't feel inclined to buy the ingredients for a meal any more. Martin lived at home but was, more often than not, at his girlfriend's. What then was the point in meticulously shopping for lots of complicated things and then spending an hour-and-a-half in the kitchen making an elaborate meal that she'd then sit and eat on her own in ten minutes. Sally had therefore entered the world of ready meals and boxed salads. And she'd explored, more deeply than before, the world of red and white wine, because that helped too.

She drove home, put the shopping away, fed the dog, fed herself on a bag of crisps and a coffee, put on her jeans and decided she'd walk the dog later. Dave had got it from a refuge without asking her first, and Sally resented it was still with her when he wasn't. She then drove to Newark's Kelham Road ground to watch Martin and the lads train. Reggie had retained some land outside the ground for the rugby club to play on and to accommodate a grass training pitch for the football team. It also had a five-a-side Astroturf pitch, and the whole training area had floodlights.

As Sally pulled up in the car park, she could see that the players were mingling about, but there was little action. She walked over and leaned on a wall to watch what happening. Sally had often gone to training when Dave was manager, so the squad was used to seeing her, but now he'd gone she didn't want them to think she was mother hen fussing over her son. He'd get a right ribbing if they did. She used to help set out the cones, and often refereed practice matches while Dave barked out his instructions. It was second nature to her after a childhood almost living at Portman Road. She enjoyed being involved at the club and didn't see why she should stop now. It would probably be a different matter when Reggie brought in a new man.

After about ten minutes Martin jogged over.
"Alright Ma?" he asked. "Bloody shambles here."
"What's going on? This won't get you promoted. Scratching your arse and getting cold," she replied.
"Jez is here but he's badly. He's been to the bog three times already. He's told us to warm up and do some ball work 'til he comes out."
"What? Where is he?"
"Changing rooms. You're not gonna cause a fuss are you?"
"Course not. I'll go and have a word though. You've got Southport on Saturday and you should be pushing yourselves hard."
Sally walked in to the dressing room where Andy Brewer, centre-half, stood wearing only a jock strap ready to put on his training kit.
"Alright Sal, how's it going?" he asked, "I'm late but it doesn't look like I've missed anything."
"Sorry Andy, mate, don't mind me," she said, "Martin said our answer to Alex Ferguson is ill. I've just come to see if he's dead or not."
"Judging by the sounds coming out of there, I'd say death was imminent," said Andy, gesturing to the toilets.
Sally went in and crouched down to look under the cubicle doors until she could see two feet with trousers crumpled around them. She entered the next cubicle and stood on the toilet seat looking over the partition.

"What the fuck's up with you?" she asked.
"Fucking hell, make me jump why don't you. I'd shit myself if I wasn't doing that already," said Jez, sitting on the toilet. "I'm pissing out my arse, Sal. What the fuck's caused this I don't know, but I've got the worst case of the shits in history. I nearly caused a pile up on the A46 'cos I had to pull up quick and shit in the hedge."
"Well ten out of ten for getting here - but you're not a fat lot of use to those lads if you're going to be sat on the throne all evening," said Sally. "Is anyone else here that can take training?"
"Slug's here somewhere."
"Slug? He's not much cop as a physio let alone know anything about training. Oh fuck it, I'll do it. Why not. That'll be a first. Leave you too it, Jez."
"Cheers Sal. Pass another bog roll over before you go, would you."

Sally left the building and walked over to the players.
"Gather round, lads," she shouted. "Look, my shit of a husband has gone - sorry Martin, forgot you were here - and you haven't got a new gaffer yet. On top of that your caretaker boss is stuck on the shitter. I'll take the session if you like. Any objections?"
"Course not, Sal," said Jason Little, the captain. "You've always done OK when you helped Dave. Go for it. Alright lads?" and the squad all muttered their agreement.
"OK, get yourselves on to that Astroturf," said Sally.

• • •

"If you want that shag you better hurry up."
"Why? You don't need to open early."
"Yes I bloody do," said Angie, United's social club stewardess. "Your boring bloody supporters' club have got a quiz on tonight. They'll be here at seven and all I'll hear all night is 'which footballer's name is an anagram of 'arsehole'?' or 'name the deepest lake in the Lake District' and all that rubbish. Load of boring bloody anoraks in here for hours."
"What - there's a player whose anagram of his name is 'arsehole'? Bloody hell," said Reggie.
"Of course not, I'm speaking figuratively, you prawn. And I'm not

doing it on the pool table again. We'll do it in the committee room on your posh table."
"Your wish is my command, gorgeous."

Since Reggie's wife left him he'd spent even more time with Angie than usual. They'd been having an affair for months, and he often called in to the club to see her before driving home to Nottingham. He didn't want it to develop into something more serious but having sex with her took his mind off his troubles. Angie knew this and was a willing partner. She first gave in to his advances because he owned the club and the takings weren't good so she wanted to keep him happy. She thought he was an old fool and a soft touch, but just lately she wondered if she could replace Deirdre in his life, with all the trappings that would bring. They left the bar area and went into the committee room across the corridor.

He kissed her and slid his hand under her blouse. She unbuckled his belt and pulled down his zip. He turned her around and lowered her onto the oak table, pulling her skirt up around her waist at the same time.
"This isn't a bloody sex show, for god's sake," said Angie.
"What?"
"Close the bloody blind. Anyone can see in here, you pillock."
Reggie shuffled over to the window, his trousers round his ankles.
"My God!" he exclaimed. "I don't believe it."
"What are you gawping at? Come back over here. I told you I haven't got all night," said Angie.
"Over there on the training pitch. The lads training. And Sally's taking it. She's bloody taking training!"
"So she's more interesting than me, is she? Well, you can stuff getting your end away. Are you listening? Oh, for god's sake. I'm going to finish the sandwiches," said Angie, as she adjusted her clothes before storming out of the room, slamming the door behind her. Reggie slowly pulled up his trousers and tucked in his shirt as he stood at the window absorbed by what he could see.
"And she looks pretty bloody good at it too," he said to himself, as he zipped up his fly.

At nine o'clock, Sally finished the session and the squad trooped off towards the changing rooms. She walked behind them and Jason paused to speak to her.
"Thanks Sal, that was good. Not too heavy, but good," he said.
"How do you mean, Jase?" she asked.
"Well, don't get me wrong, I'm not taking sides, but your old man used to kill us. We'd be completely shagged out by the time we'd finished."
"Yeah, and how many times were you sluggish on a Saturday? My dad always used to say 'keep something in reserve'. Go so far in training, but not too far. Save it for when you need it. And I don't just mean energy. I mean desire as well."
"Fair comment Sal," said Jason, "fair comment."
Sally then caught up with Danny Thomas. He was only seventeen and had signed for Newark after impressing in the local leagues.
"You OK, Danny?" she asked.
"Yeah, not bad, Mrs Hampton, not bad," he replied. "Bit pissed off with my form, but I'll keep trying."
"That might be the problem Danny, trying too hard. Play the easy ball a few times. Don't always look for the match-winning pass. The miracle passes don't often come off. And another thing I've noticed. You're a tall lad for a midfielder. Good thing that, when it comes to getting from box to box, 'cos you can cover the ground. But when you've got the ball, well, standing tall isn't so good. Crouch a bit. Lower your centre of gravity. You'll be quicker on your feet and you'll be able to go one side or the other better. Just try it. Stoop a bit. Bend your knees."
"OK Mrs H. Thanks, I'll think about that," said Danny.
"Well done, mum, you did well," said Martin as he stood with Sally outside the dressing room door. "The lads enjoyed it. And Jase has just said you know what you're talking about."
"I enjoyed it too," she said. "You'd got no-one to take training, so I took my chance. Let's hope you guys take your chances at Southport on Saturday. I'm off. See you later."
"Yeah, see you at home, Capello," said Martin, and he winked at her before joining the others inside.

• • •

"Come on then. Show us what you've got," said Reggie. It was eleven o'clock and he had been joined by Darren, the young sales rep from Gift Solutions UK (Scunthorpe branch). They supplied a lot of his stock and Reggie prided himself on spotting a winning line.

"What about this Reggie?" said Darren as he took a combined ashtray/radio/toilet roll holder out of its box.

"No, I don't think so, son. Too many people giving up fags these days. Bloody smoking ban. When it comes to smoking-related stuff, it's killing my takings. Even the sort who go on their hols to the east coast are packing in. Next?"

"This is going down well. Sold over five thousand so far," said Darren as he unveiled a mirror engraved with a man's bearded face.

"Who the hell is it?" asked Reggie.

"David Beckham, Reggie, can't you see?"

"David Beckham? It looks more like bloody Osama Bin Laden. You'll have to do better than that."

"OK Reggie, here goes, the piece de resistance. Hang on, let me get it out. There, take a look at this. It's switched on. Clap your hands." In front of Reggie an eighteen-inch high plastic judge, complete with wig and gown, stood on his desk. He clapped his hands and the learned figure broke into a tinny rendition of "I Fought the Law". As the song reached its climax, the judge's stern face changed to a leering grin. On the last note, he leaned back and opened his gown to reveal a huge erection. Darren convulsed with laughter.

"Brilliant hey, Reggie? I'll leave you this one. Amuse your staff."

"I'll take a thousand. They'll sell well. Especially in Skegness," said Reggie.

The paperwork done, Darren left and Sue, Reggie's secretary, brought in some mail for him to read. He sat back at his desk and idly flicked through a catalogue. He was pleased Darren had visited his office because it took his mind off a series of depressing matters. He was still deeply angry his wife had left him, and he knew he was neglecting to spend enough time running his business. He also knew he was taking too long to recruit a new manager for the football club. On top of all that he was very upset he'd missed out on a shag with Angie last night. Then the phone rang.

"Call for you on line one, Reggie," said Sue.

"Oh, I'm not in the mood for any calls, sweetheart, tell 'em I'm out," he replied.
"It's your wife."
"What!" said Reggie, sitting upright. "Put her through."
"Right, Reggie. I'm not having a long discussion," said Deirdre. "I want half the house and half the business. You can keep your bloody football club. Get your solicitors on to it."
"This is the first time we've spoken since you ran off with that louse, and that's all you've got to say," said Reggie. "After all those years together. Come home love, please."
"Don't give me all that. You didn't know I existed while you were busy selling tat and spending all your time at that bloody football ground. You should have given me a bit of attention. I've got a new life now. Anyway, I hear you've been spending plenty of time with Dave's ex. I'm sure she's bloody comforting you. The tart."
"Hang on a minute. I don't believe this. You're JEALOUS!"
"Don't bloody flatter yourself. I've got to go. Got customers to serve. Get your solicitor's arse in gear. You hear me?" and with that Deirdre hung up. Reggie slowly replaced the phone. After all that had happened, he thought to himself, his wife was actually jealous that he'd been seen out with another woman. He smiled to himself and clapped his hands. The words "I fought the law and the law won" rang out from across the office as the judge burst into song.

• • •

"Indicate, you shit! Jesus Christ! I'm not a fucking mind reader. Wanker!" shouted Terry, the coach driver. The team were returning from Southport where they'd won 1- 0 through an Andy Brewer header on seventy-five minutes.

The journey home was enjoyable because of the result and Terry's constant griping at other motorists had been drowned out by the players singing and laughing. Most of the squad knew that Terry was possibly the worst person to have taken up driving for a living. They were amazed at his ability to be permanently aggressive. Usually, they sniggered in the back of the bus while it went on for mile after mile, but today they were elated at their performance and his ranting was mostly ignored. Jason sat on his own at the front of the coach. He'd had a good game and he felt he was justifying his selection as captain. He been chosen for the role at the start of the season and he thought it had helped develop his overall game. He wanted to be on his own for an hour or so though, because he wanted to think a few things through.

"Stick in your fucking lane, you arse!" said their driver, interrupting Jason's thoughts. He had noticed the players' anxiety about the time it was taking to appoint a new manager. He was also worried that Reggie might bring in the wrong guy, just when the season was going well and they were picking up points each week. On top of everything, Jason had a pretty radical idea that, if he voiced it, might alienate him from the rest of his team mates. At that moment, he decided that he'd go for it.

"Fuck off, dickhead! Go fuck yourself!" shouted Terry, as he waved a V sign out of the driver's side window.

"Christ, Terry, you'll have a bloody heart attack," said Jason, as he stood up and went to the back of the coach.

He got the players' attention. "Hey lads, I want a word with you when we get back. Most of us are getting off at Castle Donnington. We'll go in the hotel bar there and have a natter. And then a few beers."

• • •

"Hi Angie, you OK?" asked Sally as she walked through the social club.

"Yeah, fine pet. You're looking well," replied Angie, as she wiped the bar.

"I'm here to see Reggie. Don't know what he wants. Probably going to try and get his hands on my arse again! Only joking."

"Many a true word," said Angie, suppressing her irritation. "He's in the committee room with the rest of the guys. They're waiting for you."

"Rest of the guys? This is odd. See you in a bit."

Sally walked through to the committee room, knocked on the door, and entered.

"Hello Sally. Come in," said Reggie who gestured towards the chair facing the group of men at the table. "I think you know these fellas. Our committee - Tom to my right, Dean and Walter to my left. You're probably wondering what on earth all this is about."

"Well, yes. I feel like I'm at a job interview. Only I haven't applied for one."

"Well, to be honest Sal, you're not far off. I've been talking to the guys here over the last couple of days. I've had an idea. It involves you. What swung it was Jason ringing me on behalf of the players. Seems he's had the same idea too. We need a manager and we want it to be you. What do you think?"

"What!" said Sally. "Are you mad? Why me?"

"Because we all know you know your stuff. The players respect you. They always have. You took training and you were excellent. Your father was a legend and you've learned from him. And from Dave."

"I learned a lot from my dad and sod all from Dave. Sorry. What about my job in the bank?"

"We want you full time. Leave the bank. We'll pay you what you get there plus half as much again and we'll supply you with a car. What do you reckon? Are you game? Do you need time to think about it?"

"No, I'll do it. And I'll bloody do it well. I'll be your new manager," said Sally, smiling.

Reggie opened the door and shouted some instructions to Angie. Seconds later, she joined them with a bottle of champagne and they celebrated her appointment. As Sally spoke to the others about having a meeting with the players, Tom whispered to Reggie "You're not shagging her - are you, chairman?"

"Sadly not, Tom. Sadly not," he replied. That certainly isn't the motive for giving her the job, he thought to himself. Getting back at Deirdre and making her even more jealous might have something to do with it though. And, he thought, if it helps win her back and, even more importantly, stops him losing half his business and half his house, then it could be the best thing he'd done for a long time.

The players sat in their training kit in the dressing room fidgeting around. They'd been summoned to a meeting with their new manager an hour before training, and they were eager to hear what she'd got to say. They'd grilled Martin with question after question about his mother becoming their boss, but he knew little more than they did. Sally walked in and addressed them.

"Right guys," she said, "your new coach will be joining us when we start training. He's called Bernie and you're to do everything he says. He was a player at Ipswich under my dad and he's a top coach. I've known him for years and he's going to help me as a favour until the end of the season. He does all the fitness stuff and you'll find out how lucky you are, 'cos you'll feel in the best shape possible after a few sessions. Now, most of all, you'll want to know what I'm going to bring to the party. First and foremost, we're going to play in a new pink strip. And to attract more women fans you're going to wear much shorter shorts. Oh, and before I forget, we're going to have some nice looking male cheerleaders. God, your faces - I'm JOKING, you wallies!"

The players all relaxed and laughed embarrassedly.

"I'm going to keep it simple because football is a simple game. It's all about movement. You move with the ball - into space. You move without the ball - marking the opposition and closing them down. The team that's the most mobile and moves best wins. When we need to, we do things fast. And when we need to slow things down, that's what we do. I'll have no favourites and what's best for the team is what's best for me. That'll do for now but I've got lots of ideas I'll introduce over the next few weeks. Any questions?"

"No, that's great. We're pleased you're our new boss," said Jason, "and we'll do everything you say."

"That's great," said Sally. "We can win this league and we'll give it our best shot. Now there's one last thing I need to get out the way. It's to do with me being a woman and you being blokes and the fact that I'm gonna be in here with you match after match. I don't want it to be an issue."

With that Sally took off her T-shirt and slipped off her jogging bottoms. She stood in front of them naked.

"Mum! What the bloody hell are you doing?" said Martin, purple with embarrassment.

"Sorry, son, but I know what I'm doing. OK guys, I've got nice tits, my belly is a bit flabby, and I've got stretch marks on my arse. Take a good look." With that she paused for a couple of seconds.

"Right. Now it's your turn. Get your kit off. Go on. Get your tackle out." The players slowly took off their training gear.

"OK, let's see," said Sally. "A few good ones and one or two acorns."

Some of the players moved their hands in front of themselves, defensive-wall-style.

"OK lads, that'll do, get dressed," said Sally, as she put her clothes back on. "Before you think I'm some sort of exhibitionist, I was absolutely dreading doing that. But I thought it would solve something once and for all. So no need for any awkwardness in the dressing room from now on. Winning is all we need to think about. Now off you go. Bernie should be outside waiting for you and I'll join you when he's got you warmed up."

The players trooped out into the cold night air.

"You were right," said Danny, as he walked past. "Nice tits, Sally."

"It's not Sally, it's 'boss'," she said.

"Sorry. Nice tits, boss."

"Get out of here," said Sally smiling, and she pushed him out the door.

• • •

In the short time leading up to Sally's first game as manager, she vowed she would abide by a series of rules she'd made for herself. These included being honest with the players, not getting into any sort of slanging match with an opposing manager, respecting the officials, and keeping calm under all circumstances. Driving to the ground, she repeated these vows over and over to remember them. Fifteen minutes into the match, she'd broken every one. And as Newark were 2-0 up by then, she didn't give a shit.

She announced the line-up in the dressing room before the game, and explained that she'd made one or two changes. Eddie Walker was left out, and he clearly took it badly. Sally noted this and took him to one side as the players went out on to the pitch. She told him he was due a rest so he'd be on the bench for a couple of games, and then she'd look at bringing him back. She'd really dropped him because she was never convinced he was good enough, and he'd be moved to another club if the chance came. Newark scored a cracking goal after five minutes and were awarded a penalty three minutes later. The opposing manager strode along the touchline enraged by the decision and ranted at Sally about her player diving. She told him where to go and, when he continued to hurl abuse, she told him to cool down and squirted him with water from a drinks bottle; an action that brought loud cheers from the fans behind them. Jason Little took the penalty and their keeper saved it. Sally strode on to the pitch shouting to the referee, convinced the goalkeeper had moved before the kick was taken. As the assistant referee pulled her back to the touchline, she told him the referee was a 'bloody muppet' for not seeing what had happened until she realised he had, and the penalty was already being retaken and converted. As Newark clung on for a 2-1 win and the players came off the pitch elated, Sally realised it was pointless making her own rules. She had to play by the rules everyone else played by. Except, she vowed, she'd be better at it than everyone else.

In the changing room, Sally addressed the players as a group and then went round speaking to them individually. Bernie told them about arrangements for their midweek game at Solihull Moors. Just then Reggie burst in and asked Sally to go with him to the committee room.
"The media want to see you, Sal. I want to make the most of the attention. Good bit of PR for the club, all this," he said.
"I'll come, but only because I've finished with the players, Reggie," said Sally. Taking him to one side she added, "It might be your club, but in future you only come in here when I say so. The dressing room is mine. It's an important part of what I do with the players."
"OK, keep your hair on. The business side of the club is mine. If I can get this club some exposure, I will. It can lead to more money in the till. And a lot of that money goes on those lads. Now come on, there's loads of media here. Never seen anything like it."
Reggie escorted Sally to the committee room where she found radio and newspaper reporters and photographers waiting for her. Reggie introduced her to them and persuaded her to stand in front of a display screen. The photographers flashed their cameras, and she noticed that the backcloth behind her was emblazoned with the words 'Grainger's Quality Fancy Goods.'
"Good for the club, my arse," said Sally to Reggie.
The reporters started to fire questions at her.
"Hold on, hold on," she said, as she moved towards them. "Before we go any further, I've got a question for you lot. Here you all are

- from 5 Live, the Guardian, all sorts of places. I want to know why the hell are you all here? I'll answer that question for you. 'Cos I'm a bloody woman, that's why. And that's a sad indictment of the football industry, if you ask me. So from now on you ask me about the team, the game, whatever. I'm the manager and those questions are fine. But you ask any questions about me being a woman manager and you'll get a simple two-word answer. And the second word is 'off'. I hope I've made myself clear."
"OK, ladies and gentlemen," said Reggie. "I think you can see we got ourselves an exceptional new manager and this club is going places. If you'd like to ask your questions then please fire away, but first of all can I ask that you take a few more photos."
As he spoke he put his hands on Sally's shoulders and gently guided her back in front of the advertising screen.
"Get those cameras working everyone. Fantastic," said Reggie.
"And we've also got an exceptional bullshitter of a chairman," Sally whispered to him, before she started to answer their questions.

On the journey to the Midlands for their Tuesday evening game, Sally's mobile phone rang.
"Sal, it's Reggie. Good luck tonight. Sorry I can't be with you."
"Thanks, Reggie," she replied. "Tough game, but I reckon we can get a result."
"Good lass. Just one thing. I got a call from Marriotts this morning. They've got a bill outstanding for last month's coaches for our away games. I'd overlooked paying it. Bill Marriott told me the bill will be way higher from now on. What's all that about?"
"Quite simple, Reggie. The players have been going to away games in a bloody death trap. Not only that but it'd got no toilet and no microwave."
"Well we're only non-league Sal. We're not Chelsea."
"I don't care," retorted Sally. "These players are working lads. Some of them have been at work today. Andy's been sorting letters since four this morning. They need to relax and eat something. Not arrive there and try and play after being cramped up on a bloody clapped out ex-school bus for hours. I've sorted them something decent to ride in."

"And muggins here has to pay for it," said Reggie. "I hope you're not going to be like all the others, Sal. Want, want, want."

"Well, here's some more news for you. I've just transferred Eddie Walker to Gainsborough. That's £320 a week I've just saved you. Whoever agreed to pay him that wants their head examining."

"That was your ex. Well done, Sal. Top stuff."

"I'll ring you after the game. From the new bus," said Sally.

In the dressing room, the players waited until it was time to get changed by flicking through the programme or chatting amongst themselves. Sally used this time to assess them. She wanted to see if they all got on, or if there were some cliques that excluded other teammates. She was pleased that, so far, they all seemed to be good friends and the spirit was good. She'd known of teams that didn't perform on the pitch because of animosity off it, despite the players being, on paper, much more skilled than a lot of their opponents. Most of all she wanted to see the 'look' on their faces. She wanted to see if they looked natural and at ease or if they were just acting the role of footballer and hiding their real feelings.

The most obvious example of this was the player left out of the starting eleven. He would act supportive of those who were playing and appear outwardly relaxed - when his 'look' clearly showed he resented being excluded, and all he wanted was to be somewhere else. Sally first noticed that look when, as a youngster, she watched the Cup Final on television. The players left out, having sat through the whole match in their club suits, rushed to congratulate their winning team mates at the final whistle. They smiled and laughed and hugged their pals, but if the chance had come to leave the stadium and drive away, some of them would have grabbed it with both hands. She also remembered seeing that look years ago when she took Martin to play group and stayed to help. She'd notice any little mite who'd been left there by a working mum or dad and who quite simply wanted to be at home. Players pretending to be part of a happy squad instead of genuinely feeling involved and vowing to win a place back in the team were better off not being there. She knew she'd always have to keep watching for the signs.

The first half was a tight affair with few chances created by either team. Sally was pleased Newark went in at half-time all square but she was worried that if they conceded first, they'd struggle to impose themselves and get back into the game. As the players left the pitch at the break she followed them, talking to Bernie.
"Get your tits out, get your tits out, get your tits out for the lads," sang a group of home fans near the changing rooms.
"Get yours out; they're bigger," said Sally to one of them, who was clearly overweight. This caused his pals to divert their attention from her to him and they ribbed him mercilessly.
"You'll soon get sick of that sort of thing," said Bernie.
"It's OK. I had a bet with my mate Denise how long it'd take to hear that one. It's only taken a game and a half, so I win," said Sally. "Anyway, I'm not happy with that display. We need some pace up front. And we need to get behind their defence. What do you reckon?"
"Yeah, I agree boss," said Bernie.

After an hour, Sally made a couple of changes but her team still didn't pose a threat to the home side's goal. Almost inevitably, Solihull scored and despite pushing their centre-half up, Newark couldn't find an equaliser. With a few minutes to go, the referee missed an obvious foul and Sally protested from the touchline.
"Shut your face, you fucking bitch," said the Solihull full-back, as he jogged back into position.

At the final whistle, with Newark having lost 1-0, Sally walked across to her opposite number near the home dugout. She shook hands with him and told him his side deserved it on the night.
"Thanks. Your lot were unlucky," he said. "And I'm sorry for the stick you got. Especially near the end. I'll be kicking his arse for that."
"No, don't," said Sally. "He'll think I've complained. But thanks for apologising on his behalf. Good luck until we play you at our place."

On the coach on the way home, Sally rang Reggie and he read out the rest of the results from their league. Newark had dropped a place but were still around halfway in the table. Sally chatted to Bernie and they agreed that staying in Blue Square North would be a good achievement after their speedy rise up the leagues. Privately, she thought that they might just sneak into the play-offs, and, if so, she'd have proved that she had what it takes to be a successful manager.

• • •

On Wednesday and Thursday, Sally spent her time at the ground. As well as team matters, she helped with commercial activities at the club; something a lot of full-time non-league managers did, whose players were only part time. She spoke to the shirt sponsors and had a meeting with the owner of a local company who was interested in taking over as main sponsor. On Thursday evening, the players had a full training session. For a change, they trained with the reserve squad and Sally suggested to Grant McBride, their coach, that they had a combined session more often. The dour Scot was less than enthusiastic. It seemed pretty clear, as she'd already been warned, that he was still uneasy about her being the new manager. She wasn't particularly concerned, but knew that this was something that would need to be resolved if she was going to manage the football side of the club properly.

Friday was a day off and Sally caught up with a lot of household chores. She also took the dog to the vet, cursing all the way there and all the way home, unhappy that she was still responsible for it. At four, she picked up Denise and they went for a drink at her favourite pub, deep in the Nottinghamshire countryside. Dave and Sally used to take Martin there when he was a young lad. They walked through the pub and went into the beer garden at the rear.
"It's glorious here," said Sally. "Martin used to love running around in this garden. Look at the views. The woods in the distance. And the sheep grazing over the fence. It's idyllic."
"It is, Sal. This'll be a nice break from football for you. How's it going?" asked Denise.
"It's going fine. I'm loving it. Reggie is …..well, Reggie. He tells me to do this and do that and I nod my head. Then I do it my way. The players are great. They're a great team. It's good."
"How are you being treated? It's obviously very much a male world

you're in. What's it like?"

"If I thought of some of the things that are said to me or that I've overheard, I'd explode. But if I think about things like that and react, it's the team that suffers. I only suffer if the team does. I'm not bothered about me."

"I've got a surprise for you," said Denise. "I've set up a supporters' trust. We've got a working party and, up to now, we've got over a hundred members lined up. We've said it's £25 minimum to join and so far we've had over four grand pledged in subscriptions and donations."

"That's fantastic Dee," said Sally. "Brilliant. But don't let Reggie get his mitts on it. He'll blow it on something stupid like a new drinks cabinet in the committee room."

"Don't you worry. It's all going to you. Add it to your budget. That's what we've decided."

"Fantastic. I've got my eye on a striker who's out of favour at Notts. He's like greased lightening. They'll keep paying most of his wages but your money will mean I can have him 'til the end of the season."

Just then a girl walked through the garden towards them carrying plates of food. Another followed with cutlery, a bottle of wine, and two glasses.

"Where did all this come from?" asked Sally.

"Another surprise," said Denise, "I ordered it on the way in. You deserve it after all your hard work."

Sitting at a wooden table, the two women tucked in. They chatted about family, friends, and football. Denise asked Sally if she'd got herself a new bloke.

"Not yet," said Sally. "I'm not in a mad rush. And before you ask, I don't fancy any of the players. That wouldn't be a great move. I reckon a few of them would like to get off with me though, even though I'm way older. Just so they could say they'd pulled the manager."

As she spoke, Sally left her seat and walked the short distance to the fence. She held out a lettuce leaf and a sheep came over and took it.

"It really is lovely and peaceful here," she said, stroking it.

Just then a Mercedes tore into the overspill car park alongside the

beer garden. It screeched to a halt in the gravel and as the doors opened, loud music blared out. Two smartly dressed young men climbed out and walked into the pub laughing and swearing loudly.
"Spoke too soon," said Sally. "Arseholes!"
Sally poured Denise more wine and they talked about the new trust. Denise explained that she thought it would be fantastic if Newark's fans owned the football club and representatives from the supporters and the business community ran it.
"Nothing against Reggie," she said, "because he's ploughed a lot of money in setting up the club. But that isn't a long-term thing. We reckon loads more people would contribute if they all had a stake in things."
"You're right. Reggie has been brilliant, even if he is an old lech," said Sally, "but his head is all over the place since Deirdre went awol. Some of the people who use the bank might be interested too. Maybe you could set up a fans' meeting. I'll come with our captain. Let's build up a bit of momentum."
"Good idea. Anyway, I need the ladies. I'll be back in a minute."
"Hang on. It's getting a bit chilly. Let's go and sit inside," said Sally.
With that, the two women walked back into the pub. Denise found the ladies and Sally walked into the lounge. The pub was fairly busy and she bought a tonic water for herself and another glass of wine for Denise.

Denise returned and they found a table where they continued to talk about the club.
"You're that football woman, aren't you?"
Sally looked up to see one of the loud young men speaking to her.
"If you mean I'm the manager of Newark, you're spot on," she replied, smiling.
"I'm Lee. I was on the books at Forest. Knee injury meant I had to pack in, otherwise I'd be there now. That's right, ain't it, Wayne?"
His friend standing unsteadily at the bar nodded in agreement.
"You look a bit tasty. Better than your pictures in the Advertiser," he went on. "You fancy a drink? Us two and you two make a four. We've had a good day at Southwell races. Celebrate with us."
"Thanks, but no thanks, we're off in a minute," said Denise.

"Come on, let's have some fun," he said, as he leaned over towards them, spilling his drink on the carpet. "Can't be that often you two get asked out by two good-looking young blokes like us."
"No really, it's OK. We've got to go," said Sally.
"I get it, you're 'together'. Not interested in blokes. That's why you're a manager. 'Cos you bat for the other side. We'll leave you to it, girls."
Sally and Denise smiled at each other and picked up their things as the young man joined his friend back at the bar. They walked towards the door.
"Just a minute, Dee," said Sally, and she walked back over to the two men.
"Lee, honey, I've been thinking about what you said. You're a good-looking lad. I've never done anything like this before," she said. Then she leaned over and whispered in his ear: "I want to satisfy you. Give me your car keys. Give me five minutes and then come round the back. You'll have the best time you've ever had. Make sure it's five minutes though, or the deal's off. I need time to get ready."
Lee, beaming, handed over his keys and nudged his mate violently.
"Fucking hell, I knew she was up for it," he told him.
Sally rejoined Denise near the door.
"You're surely not interested in that moron?" asked Denise, shocked.
"Wait in the car, I won't be long," replied Sally, handing over her own car keys.
"I don't believe this," said Denise.
With that the two women left the pub, Denise walking out the front door towards her friend's car, and Sally going back towards the garden.

Two or three minutes later, Denise saw Sally jog up the driveway at the side of the building towards her. She leaned across and opened the driver's side door allowing her to jump into her seat.
"Give me the keys, we're off," said Sally breathlessly, as she put on her seat belt.
"What happened? You weren't long. You didn't meet that horrible git, did you?" asked Denise, as the car sped away from the pub.
"'Course I didn't," said Sally. "Give me some credit. I said he'd be

satisfied. Well, I've put something in his car for the obnoxious bastard to have his end away with. That sheep. It's on his back seat."
"You haven't? That's fantastic!"
"Yeah, it struggled a bit mind. And it must have been nervous. 'Cos what do animals do when they're nervous? It's pissed all over his upholstery."
Both women cried with laughter as they headed back towards Newark.

• • •

The following Saturday, Newark were outstanding and won at Eastwood 3-0. The result was never in doubt and they outplayed the home team from the first minute to the last. Sally was overjoyed, even though she didn't want to show it. She tried to adopt the same demeanour in front of the players, whether they won or lost. She knew that was how a good manager would deal with success or failure in any other business, and she didn't think being a football manager should be any different. After the game, Sally, Bernie, Slug and the first-team squad were dropped off in the middle of Nottingham. They filed into a pub where Sally had arranged for food and drinks to be laid on for them. The official reason for the gathering was to celebrate Jason's thirtieth birthday. This was partially true, but she also wanted to thank her captain for the support he had given her at the start of her managerial career, even though she kept this particular motive a secret from him.

Getting the players together socially after such a good win would do no harm to team spirit either. The players tucked into the buffet and bottles of lager were lined up on the bar. A few of the Nottingham-based reserves joined them and, after an hour or so, the atmosphere was good-natured and lively. The players decided to spend the evening in the town centre and go to a club later on.

"What happened outside the ground today boss?" Bernie asked Sally, as they smiled at the players horsing around and joking with each other.
"What? Oh that," she replied. "Bloody jobsworth wouldn't let me

in. I had to force him to get their secretary to prove I was with the team."
"That's out of order. They should have known you're the manager."
"All he could see was a woman trying to get into the away dressing room. That was something he couldn't get his head round. Welcome to the twenty-first century or what."
"Thick sod. You going round town with the lads?"
"Hell no. I don't think they'd welcome that, especially Martin. Anyway, I'm not feeling one hundred percent. Think I'll go home and have an early one. Watch Match of the Day and relax."
"It's not like you to complain, Sal," said Bernie. "Even with all the shit you've had."
"I'm OK. I live and breath this job. It's a dream come true. I'm just tired that's all. Nothing a good night's sleep won't solve," said Sally.

Sally was woken up by noises downstairs. Looking at her watch, she saw it was half-past-three. She put on her dressing gown and slowly crept downstairs, holding a hair dryer as a weapon. The light was on in the kitchen and through a gap in the door she could see a figure staggering around. She tiptoed to the doorway and burst in.
"If you don't get out I'll call the police…," she screamed. "…Fucking hell Martin, what the hell are you doing here? You always stay at Lyndsey's. You scared the shit out of me."
Martin turned to face her. "My god, what the hell has happened to you?" asked Sally. Her son's white shirt was covered in blood and his face was cut and swollen.
"I got in a fight. Dean and Gaz from the reserves. We were all pissed," said Martin.
"It doesn't look like a bloody fight. It looks like you got a good hiding. I'll bloody kill 'em."
"No, you can't say anything," said Martin, holding his side.
"You've hurt your ribs too, by the look of it. How did all this happen? And don't worry, I won't grass you up. Just tell me."
"They were taking the piss out of you. Said you were only manager 'cos you were sleeping with Reggie. And they said I'm only in the first team 'cos my mum picks me. Mummy's boy and all that. I twatted Gaz good and proper but the two of 'em ended up panning me."
"Come here," said Sally, and she hugged him. "You're a good lad,

standing up for me. Let's get you cleaned up. We should take you to A and E."

"I'm OK. Just a bit sore," said Martin, and she saw tears well in his eyes.

"It's been hard, the last few weeks," she said, "and me taking on your dad's job hasn't helped."

By now Martin was sobbing. "I miss my dad. And every time you do something at the club, the lads say you do it better than he did. I know he shouldn't have done what he did. Go off with another woman. But I miss him."

"I know, I know. Let's get you cleaned up. Does Lyndsey know where you are? Stay here tonight. I'll look after you."

"I texted her. Didn't want to go to hers in this state. Yeah I'd like to stay with you."

"Just remember, when I'm at the club I'm your manager, not your mum. And your father is the ex-manager, not your dad. It's different there to how it is at home. And you get in the team through merit. Why don't you have next week off? Go to Spain to see him. Have some time with your father," said Sally, wiping the tears from his face.

"What, and miss a match? No way," said Martin.

She hugged her son even tighter.

• • •

Sally sat in her office at the ground. She'd been working there all day, and later they were playing Stafford Rangers in a re-arranged fixture. She wasn't happy about having to play another midweek game but there was nothing she could do about it. Anyway no one had reported in injured after the Eastwood game, so she had a fit squad to chose from. Ironically, of everyone connected with the club, it was the manager who wasn't well. Her aches and pains from the weekend had developed into a severe bout of flu, but she wasn't going to let that get in the way of doing everything it took to get another three points on the board that evening. Just then the phone rang.

"Sally, it's Reggie."

"Hi Reg. I'll be seeing you later. Is it anything urgent? I've got loads to do before kick off."

"I want to talk to you privately. A match night isn't the time for that so I thought I'd speak to you now. I want to talk about your son."
"Martin? Why are you ringing about Martin?" she asked.
"I've had Grant on. He's not happy about your lad. Says he's a troublemaker," said Reggie. "He told me your lad was shooting his mouth off on Saturday. I don't want to have to discipline him, Sal. Not when he's the manager's son."
"You don't need to. He's done nothing wrong. You need to sort out Grant's lads. For one, they don't know how to behave, and secondly they're crap. None of them are good enough to push for a place in the first team and that's no good to me."
"Grant's been with us a long time. He's been in the game for thirty years. I trust what he says, Sally. Speak to Martin. Sort it out."
"OK, I get it," said Sally angrily. "You trust that useless fucker and you don't trust me."
"There's no need to be like that, Sally," said Reggie.
"Fuck off, Reggie," shouted Sally, and she slammed the phone down.

Sally gave the players their team talk before kick-off but they could tell she wasn't herself. Her comments lacked any of her humour and she didn't seem to have her mind on the job at hand. Conversely, because they sensed she was troubled by something, the players' loyalty spurred them into putting their all into the match. Even so, against the run of play, Newark conceded a soft goal. Sally barked encouragement and instructions as usual, but her throat was sore, and by half-time her voice was reduced to a whisper. Stafford were riding high in the league and they held on to their 1-0 lead until the break. As the players trooped off, Sally followed the referee into his room.
"You're not allowed in here, you know that," he said.
"I know," she said. "I just want to know why you're letting them time-waste this early on in the game. Their 'keeper has been holding the ball for over ten seconds. They're taking forever over everything. I hope you're going to get them to keep the game moving after the break."
"I allowed three minutes this half. There was only one goal, no bookings and no subs. I know what I'm doing."

"OK. I just wanted to check. Thanks," said Sally as she left the room and went into the corridor.

"I see. It's true, what they say," said the Stafford assistant manager from the away team's doorway. "Using your feminine charms are you? Buttered him up so you get all the decisions. You're a disgrace, you slapper."

"Fuck you," Sally croaked. "Concentrate on your own job, arsehole." With that, she joined her team in their dressing room and spoke to them as best she could.

In the second half, Newark were on top without really troubling the Stafford keeper. Sally stood on the edge of her technical area willing her lads on. She felt ill, her team was losing, she was angry about the incident at half-time, and she was livid with her chairman for siding with the reserve team manager. In the eightieth minute, Martin was elbowed off the ball. He grabbed the offender by the throat and was about to strike him before Jason stopped him. By then, virtually all the players had got involved. The referee waited for things to calm down before calling Martin over to show him the red card. He obviously hadn't seen the first incident. Martin trooped off past his mother with his head bowed. Sally felt cold. She wondered why she was there. Before she knew it, there were tears streaming down her cheeks. She stood close to the pitch with her back to the crowd and, unbeknown to all of them, she cried her eyes out. The players battled away on the pitch in front of her so they didn't notice either. This was the most visible part of her very public job and yet no-one knew or, even less, cared how she felt. It seemed, through no fault of her own, everything was against her. There in the spotlight, she realised she'd never felt more lonely in her whole life.

Suddenly, she heard a roar from the crowd. Danny Thomas was clean through, bearing down on the Stafford goal. He was running at pace with two defenders chasing him. The advancing keeper slid towards him and, a split second before they both collided, Danny lifted the ball over him and it rolled slowly over the line into the net. Half the Newark players ran over to Danny and dived on him. The rest of the team ran across to Sally and hugged her, nearly knocking her over. With seconds to go, her team had got a point out of nowhere and it felt like a win. Sally was delighted for the players. In all the excitement, she was momentarily lost amongst them. All she hoped was that the players hadn't noticed that she'd been crying.

When she woke up next morning, Sally decided she'd spend the day at home. Other than agreeing to be interviewed by the local sports reporter, she wanted a day away from the responsibility of being a football manager. She was still feeling under the weather, but this wasn't the reason she was having a break. She needed to think about the things she'd had to put up with in her brief time in charge of the team.

She didn't know if it was because she was a woman that she'd had things said to her, or if it was because football people picked on things that were different to try and unsettle their rivals. Like if an opposing manager was fat or bald. Undoubtedly though, many of the people she had encountered had thought of her as an impostor and a threat to their masculine world. And, without doubt, a lot of the things she'd said, and the points she'd tried to make, needed to be said twice as forcibly and twice as convincingly to be accepted. That was why Reggie had so readily believed what his reserve team manager had said before he'd even heard his first team manager's point of view. One thing reassured her, though. She'd always studied football and, because of her dad and her husband, she'd considered herself to be a football person. Someone 'in' football, not just someone on the outside looking in. And in all those years, let alone in the few weeks she'd actually been in charge of a team, she knew there was one constant that never changed. And that constant was the absolute SHIT people talked about the game. They all did it - the manager talking manager-speak into a microphone, the obsessed phone-in fan who really needed to get a life, the ex-international pundit spouting complacent crap on TV, the seedy journalist wasting acres of paper on malicious rubbish, and the ego-tripping chairman posing as a leader of men who'd abandoned all business sense the minute he'd parked his fat arse in that posh seat in the main stand.

It was bound to be difficult being a woman in a man's world because that world was already full of shit. She decided the things that happened could have happened anyway, whether she'd been the archetypal white male manager or a small green alien from a faraway planet with tentacles for legs and a penis on top of her head. She decided she wouldn't let things get to her again.

• • •

Sally parked the car and checked her make-up in the mirror. She smiled to herself about the things Martin had said to her earlier. It wasn't a date she was going on, she'd told him, but he'd still warned her what might happen and what she should watch out for. She said she was only meeting an old customer from the bank, and he'd only wanted to meet her for a chat. Even so, Martin had anxiously grilled her about him. It reminded her of when he'd met Lyndsey, his first real girlfriend, and she had done the same to him.
"Hi, Sally. Good to see you."
"Hello, Steven. Nice to see you too."
He kissed her on the cheek and led her to the table in the bay window.
"Hope you don't mind. I've already asked the waiter to bring some wine. This is different from our meetings in the bank," he said.
"Yes, things have changed for me a bit. How's business?"
"Very good thanks. We're extending the factory here and are just about to sign for a new unit in the south west. It's going well. That's one of the two things I'd like to discuss with you over lunch today."
"Sounds interesting," said Sally.
They exchanged small talk and ordered lunch. Steven asked her a lot of questions about her new job. She knew he wasn't a big football fan, but he was a good listener, and she didn't feel she was boring him when she described some of things that had happened since she became manager.
"My business partner is in charge of the new factory," said Steven. "He's from this area, but he's seen the potential round there and lined up a lot of new customers. He's a big football fan too. That's why I asked to see you."
"Did I meet him at the Newark branch?" asked Sally.
"Yes, briefly. Barry came with me when we agreed new funding with your old boss. As well as the new factory, he's being persuaded to

take over as chairman at Weymouth. They've been through the mill over the last few years. He's interested and wants to help them out. They're a couple of levels lower than Newark but he thinks they can go places. They've got a decent ground. Bags of potential."

"Not being rude, but what's this got to do with me?"

"Quite a lot Sally. If he takes over at Weymouth, he wants you to be their new manager. As I say, he's a football nut. He wants to clear out all the deadwood at the club. And he's heard a lot of good things about you."

"This isn't a gimmick is it?" asked Sally "My present chairman is, shall we say, eccentric. And, between you and me, very difficult to deal with. I wouldn't want to make the same mistake."

"Barry is a clever guy. He wouldn't do anything unless it was for the right reasons."

"Well, if he's that keen, why didn't he ask me himself?"

"That's the second thing I wanted to talk to you about," said Steven. "I told him I'd like to ask you about working for him. It'd give me a chance to meet you. And ask you out for a proper date. I didn't try when you were at the bank because you were with your husband. I'd like you to come out with me. Properly next time."

"We'll see," said Sally, smiling. "On both counts."

It was a normal Thursday evening training session under lights and the players, as usual, were responding well. Sally was disillusioned with her role at the club after Reggie had let her down so badly, but she still enjoyed working with the squad. They were committed and wanted to improve. They worked on some set-plays and played defence against attack. The last half hour was spent having an eight-a-side game on a three-quarter pitch. It amused Sally that, whatever age players were, or whatever ability they had, they always wanted a competitive game at the end of a training session. She was happy to let them play as much as they wanted, as long as the tackles weren't too combative. Getting stuck in needed to be saved for the real thing.

Bernie patrolled one side of the pitch and Sally wandered over to the opposite touchline. That way, unlike on a match day, they could shout advice and instructions to players from both sides of the playing surface. Sally kept her eye on Andy, because he'd been hurt against Stafford and she wasn't sure if he was hiding an injury. He probably thought that if he could conceal it he'd have a couple of days to recover before Saturday's match at Ilkeston. He collected the ball from the keeper and went on a run down the wing.

"Man on!" shouted a voice from the gloom behind Sally, just before Andy was tackled. For a fraction of a second she felt a tingle of excitement when she heard it, just like she did years ago when she was a teenager. Then reality quickly set in and all she felt was anger.

"What the hell are you doing here?" she asked, as she looked round to see Dave leaning on the fence.

"I'm back."

"Well, I'm busy," said Sally, and she turned her attention back to her players.

After training, back in the dressing room, Sally and Bernie ran through the arrangements for meeting up on Saturday. Ilkeston was fairly local so most of the players would make their own way there. Whilst the line-up wouldn't be announced until just before kick off, Sally spent a few minutes going through what she expected of them and what they needed to look out for from one or two of the more influential Ilkeston players. As usual, Sally was the last to leave. Dave was waiting for her in the car park.

"I'm glad you're back," she told him.

"Really?" he said, eagerly.

"Yes. You can take that manky fucking dog off my hands."

"Don't be like that," said Dave.

"I hope you've spoken to Martin. You've let him down badly," said Sally.

"I've just seen him. I'm meeting him later."

"Go on then. Tell me what happened. Don't take long though, 'cos I'm not that interested. Things not so great with the lovely Deirdre then?"

"She was a nightmare. Worked with me in the bar for about a day and a half and then couldn't do it any more. Said it was too hard for her. All she was good at was lying on a sun-lounger smoking and boozing while I worked every hour god sends. Lazy cow."

"Never mind. I'm sure she was a joy to live with."

"Big mistake, the whole thing. And the health people shut the bar

down. Some customers complained. They did a surprise inspection and found cockroaches, the lot. I never thought owning a bar was that difficult."
"Well you never had any trouble being the other side of one."
"I've come back to make a fresh start. Never dreamt for a minute you'd be doing my old job," said Dave.

"Well, after going off with the chairman's wife, I wouldn't think you'd got much chance of getting it back," said Sally "Mind you, you never know with that areshole in charge. Anyway, I've got to go. I won't say it's nice to see you 'cos it isn't. Goodnight."
With that, Sally climbed in her car and drove off.

• • •

Next afternoon, Sally was in her office when she looked out the window to see Reggie's Jag screech to a halt in the car park. He jumped out of the car and trotted into the building looking flustered and hot. She heard the sounds of filing cabinets opening and slamming shut. Then he shouted down the corridor to her.
"Sally, come in here, would you. Now love. Quick as you can," he bellowed.
"Bloody hell Reggie, you're in a panic. You're sweating your cods off," she said, as she entered his office.
"I'm running late. I'm catching a plane from East Midlands and I've lost my bloody passport," he said, rummaging through his desk drawers. "I'm going to Spain to bring Deirdre back."
At that moment, Angie walked in.
"Here's the bloody Euros you asked me to get. It's not my bloody job you know, running bloody errands for you," she said as she slammed them down on to his desk, turned, and strode out again.
"Fucking hell, what's up with her? That time of the month?" said Reggie.
"Never mind that," said Sally. "They split up and you're off there like a wimp to get her back. Haven't you got a backbone?"
"Bollocks to having a backbone. It makes sense. On many levels, Sal."

"Whatever. What did you order me in here for?"

"Oh yeah, I forgot. Look, sorry but I've put Grant in charge of the first team. He's starting tomorrow at Ilkeston. You've done OK. The results have been good but that business in Nottingham wasn't great. He's experienced and………"

"Grant's players started that," Sally interrupted. "I've told you that. And he's shit. Useless. You can't do this."

"Look Sal, you must have enjoyed it. You got a lot of attention. It was good PR for the club. Never long term though. Ah, thank christ, here it is," he said, brandishing his passport. "The bank'll give you your job back. I bet they will. Or you can be Grant's assistant. Anyway, I'm late. I've gotta dash. I'll speak more about it when I get back."

And with that, he left the office and ran out of the building.

Sally walked slowly down the corridor. She was neither surprised nor upset. This was typical Reggie. She sat at her desk and looked down at the scouting report she'd been studying a few minutes earlier. She closed the folder and looked across at the team photo hanging on the wall. Those same players were now fitter than they'd ever been. They were more aware. They were a team - on and off the pitch. And they'd had some good results. She looked at Danny Thomas grinning away on the front row. She recalled how she'd given him a bit of support and a bit of advice and he'd never looked back. He was sharp and his confidence was sky high. And he'd been alert enough on Tuesday night to intercept a pass and race through to equalise. Sally thought about what she'd need to do to keep her job. She could fight to overturn the decision to replace her. And after a few seconds, she decided that would be pointless. Sally knew the job was temporary - because all managers' jobs are temporary. Everyone knows that. Except hers was always going to be more temporary. One thing she knew when she took on the manager's role was that she was never going to lose the job because she couldn't do it. She knew that if she did lose it, it would be because of stupid ignorant people. And that's exactly how it had turned out.

• • •

"Sally, it's Dave."
"How did you get this number? I changed it when you cleared off."
"I got it off Slug. I'm at Ilkeston. Thought I'd come and watch the lads."
"Well have a nice time. I'm busy. Don't phone me again."
"Martin's not here."
"He's suspended, you prat. He's with me. I'm busy. Bye."
"No, don't hang up. It's all happening here. Mega aggro," said Dave.
"What do you mean? It's only half one. The game hasn't kicked off yet," said Sally.
"The players have just been told you're sacked. They didn't know 'til now. Grant's told them he's the new boss and they don't like it."
"Well that's tough. Not my problem any more."
"Grant's handled it badly. Lost his rag and laid into them. So they won't get changed. They've told him to fuck off. They've never liked the bloke anyway, I know that. They've gone on strike, Sal."
"Well you're the big expert. You sort it out."
"They won't listen to me. I didn't just walk out on you and Martin. I walked out on them, too, don't forget. All I've been able to do is get them to stay here. And that's only 'cos I said I'd ring you."
Sally thought for a second. She thought the club had got itself into this mess and it wasn't up to her to resolve it. Then she thought about those players; how they'd become a part of her football life. She could forget getting the sack but she couldn't forget them.
"You still there, Sal?"
"I'll be there in a bit. Don't let them leave the ground," she told Dave.

"Can I help you, love? It's players and staff only through there," said the doorman in the clubhouse entrance. Sally brushed passed him.
"Don't even go there mate," said Martin, and he followed his mum down the corridor.
Grant McBride stood outside the away dressing room talking to the referee.
"What are you doing here? You've been sacked," he shouted "Get out. And take your hooligan son with you."
"You shouldn't be allowed anywhere near a football team. Fuck off

before you make things worse," said Sally. Then she opened the door and went in.

"Jesus Christ, I thought it was that prat McBride coming in again for a minute," said Jason, seeing Sally walk in. "Sorry, Sally, but he's done enough fucking damage for one day."

The Newark squad were sitting around the room. It was quarter-to-three. The kit bag lay unopened in the middle of the dressing room floor.

"Listen lads, McBride is an arse but this isn't his fault. And this isn't about me losing my job," she said. "This is the same problem that exists at clubs up and down the country. I loved being your manager. And I love this football club. But if me being given the boot helps to start sorting out its problems, then I'm glad it happened."

The players listened intently, and, apart from Sally's voice, the room was silent.

"Your chairman did well to set the club up, but it isn't healthy to have one man running it and deciding things on a whim. Cock-ups happen. And his heart isn't in it, not any more, so things were bound to go wrong. Since yesterday, I've been on the phone non-stop and had a couple of meetings. Denise and the trust and some business people might be making an offer for the club. I think Reggie will be ready to let go. And most of all, I've convinced a guy who was going to invest in another club to think about coming in with us instead. I don't know if it'll happen but it just might."

Sally gestured to Martin to come over to her.

"You're a cracking bunch of lads. You don't owe me anything. You certainly don't owe this poxy club anything. Not after what's gone on. But you can't let yourselves down and get into trouble by not playing. I've filled in a team sheet. Martin, you dash to the ref with it. He might just accept it without us getting fined." Martin left the room. "Get changed quick. Same team as Tuesday, except Alex in for Martin. Three points and we could be in the top six tonight. Get out there and stuff 'em!"

The players jumped up, tore off their clothes, and got changed. They shouted encouragement to each other and suddenly the noise in the room was deafening.

"And one more thing," shouted Sally, trying to be heard. "Watch out for their centre-half. He's a fucking animal."

Outside, Sally leaned on a rail and watched the players run out onto the pitch. She looked into the eyes of each one of them as they ran past. Of course, she had no idea what the result of the match would be. But judging by the look on their faces, she had a fair idea.

FOOTBALL BEING FOOTBALL

"You fucking lot will get me the sack. Cowards, the fucking lot of you. Not a fucking clue. I tell you all week - watch Horton peel off and come round the back. And all you fucking shower can do is ball watch. One-nil down. And you, you piece of shit, stuck on your fucking line when you should have been steaming out getting there first. Two-fucking-nil. No effort and no fucking idea. Well, I'm sick of the fucking sight of you. Sort it out yourselves. Get some pride back second half or else you're in first thing in the morning. If you ain't fucking sacked, that is. Fucking useless."

With that, manager Davie Adams left the dressing room. All was still as the players sat around the room, heads bowed. Then the silence was broken. "You out with us tonight, Hobbsy? See if we're as good on the piss as your mates at United are?" asked Shane Forbes, smiling.
"Yeah why not," said Scott Hobbs, newly signed from Manchester United. "I'll need a drink after listening to that dickhead. He wasn't like that when he was conning me into coming here on loan. Could be a long fucking month."
"He's full of shit. Take no notice," said Frankie Thomas, the captain. "All you lads out tonight then? No shirkers."
Around the dressing room, most of the players confirmed they were. One or two admitted uneasily that they couldn't make it because they were out with their girlfriends.
"Wankers," said Thomas. "What about you, Guy? You're quiet. You joining us?" "Nah, got a gig. In Lewisham," said Guy Steele, as he put his shirt back on.
"You and that fucking band. There's no hope for you," said Thomas.
"Like your fucking manager," said Hobbs.
Slowly the players rose from their seats. Keeper Aaron Jones put his gloves back on, and a couple of them loosened up and did some half-hearted stretching exercises. Then a bell rang and they slowly left the room to make their way back on to the pitch.
"Here we go lads," said Chas McDonald, in the tunnel. "Cue the fightback. Not!" and Nat Beavon next to him laughed and playfully clipped the back of his head.

The second half started and Rovers performed better. The players had little respect for their manager but subconsciously they knew they couldn't let themselves down like they did in the spell before halftime when they conceded the two goals. The defence tightened up and the midfielders and forwards upped their pace going forward. Before the match, Adams had instructed Thomas to make sure Beavon and McDonald stayed deep in midfield to stem QPR's attacking moves, but as the second period started their captain told them to "fucking go for it" and they supported the two strikers much more. They pulled a goal back from a corner when, unseen by the referee, centre-half Lee Dutton impeded their keeper and Scott Hobbs bundled the ball over the line. The last ten minutes was end-to-end and on three occasions Rangers looked like increasing their lead, only for Jones to pull off astounding saves. In the second minute of added time Adomi Kadojo, who had come on as substitute, controlled the ball on the edge of the box, turned, and curled a shot into the top corner. Most of the team jumped on top of him and the crowd went wild as Rovers gained the point that kept them in the top three in the Championship.

"You beauty," said Frankie as he wrestled Aaron Jones to the dressing room floor. His team mates were shouting and celebrating. Boots and kit were being thrown across the room and water squirted from drinks bottles. Their manager walked in and offered his hand to Frankie who shook it half-heartedly before sitting down to take off his boots.

"Glad you took notice," said Adams. "If you listen and learn, we'll be up there. Well done, lads. See you Monday." With that, he walked out into the tunnel to be interviewed by TV and radio reporters.

"Arsehole! Hey, we're in the top three, you tossers. You should be out with us tonight," said Frankie to the men who had resisted his offer at half time. "You too, Guy Fawkes. Forget frigging about playing crap music. Meet up with us - your real mates."

"Some other time Frankie," said Guy. "Can't let them down. Anyway, I enjoy it."

"You don't need to bash a guitar to pull, mate. Not when you're a Rovers' player and we're pushing for the Premier League. There'll be birds swarming all over me tonight. More fanny than I can shake a stick at."

"That's quite a picture you paint, Frankie. Enjoy."

In the car park, Guy signed autographs before climbing into his Porsche. It always amazed him how fans would hang around after a game in the hope of seeing a player and exchanging a word or two with him. He drove back to his flat, talking to his mother on the hands-free, a routine he always followed after a match. She was keen to hear how he'd played and if he had finished the game unscathed. He'd broken his leg badly when he first joined the club's academy and, ever since then, she'd scold him if he didn't let her know he was OK after a game. He didn't mind, and his mother was a good listener when he talked about the club, the manager, his team-mates, and his performances.

Guy threw his bag into the bedroom, unlocked the french doors, and stepped on to the balcony. He'd got a few minutes to collect his thoughts before heading off to Lewisham. It was cold, but he was still hot from the game. His flat was part of an exclusive development and it was popular with young professionals. In the car park below him, most of the cars had personalised number plates. He'd moved in around six months ago but he hardly knew his neighbours. Around there, people got on with leading their lives; more interested in success and money than exchanging small talk and building friendships with people they only bumped into now and again. Guy lit a cigarette and inhaled deeply. He liked smoking because it was relaxing after giving everything in a game, and it calmed him down when he wasn't training and had too much time on his hands. He tried to make sure no one knew he smoked and at home he'd brush his teeth after each cigarette. He suspected, though, that the smell took more than toothpaste to be removed from his breath and his clothes. He was as sure as anything that his mother knew he was a smoker. He thought about the game. He'd played OK. He always played OK. He was a skilful footballer and he'd got pace. His youth team coach told him it was a combination that would take him to the top, because not many players had got both artistry and speed. But it was a team game and he had to contribute physically too. Tackling, helping his full-back, defending when they were under the cosh. He wasn't good at any of those and he'd often get a roasting from his captain or his manager if they wanted to blame someone when they'd conceded a bad goal. And he wasn't strong mentally either. Some players would have a nightmare game and no one would dare to say anything. Other players attracted vitriol and they couldn't give it back. Winning the game was the only way it wouldn't happen to him, and then it didn't matter if he'd played well or badly. Guy looked at his watch, threw his cigarette from the balcony, put on jeans and a tee shirt, and sped off to the gig.

The band played well and the atmosphere was good. Singer Zoe was backed by Guy on guitar, her partner Suzi on bass, and young Joe on drums. Guy had to provide both rhythm and lead so he had a lot to do to make each song work, but he enjoyed the challenge. He found gigs like these as demanding as playing in a match. He would sweat as much too. When the kids in front of him started to move and get more and more responsive, it gave him as much of a thrill as it did when he beat a defender and smashed the ball into the back of the net. Music and football served to divert Guy from all the things that he struggled to deal with. The hours of spare time that he couldn't fill. The emptiness of living on his own. The act he had to put on. When he was a footballer on the pitch, or a musician on the stage, he was the same as the other players and the other members of the band. There was no time for people to ask questions or to be suspicious. They were all getting on with what they had to do and nothing else mattered. And when it went well, they all had a bond. He'd get a wink from a team-mate or Zoe would turn around and flash a smile at him. Nothing away from performing on a pitch or a stage could match that.

• • •

Next morning, Guy got up, made a coffee, and took it onto the balcony where he lit a cigarette. Sundays were the days that got him down. It was nine o'clock and he'd got nothing planned. When the gig finished last night he'd suggested to the rest of the band that they met up for a practice session. He suggested this because he enjoyed it when they tried new numbers and it would give him something to do. His fellow band members were less than enthusiastic and they gave him a series of excuses why they couldn't do it. He imagined what some of his team-mates would be doing. Most of them would have hangovers and a lot of them would meet up at lunchtime for the 'hair of the dog'. Others would lounge about all morning until their girlfriends or wives managed to get them to do something or go out somewhere. Without exception, none of them would be anxious about having a day off after a hard game. Only Guy did that.

He rang his mum. It would soon be Christmas and he asked her if she wanted to go shopping. She told him that she was under the weather and was staying in. Sensing the disappointment in his voice, she suggested he rang Jacqui, his sister - she had just dumped her latest boyfriend and she might be persuaded to go with him. Surprisingly, Jacqui agreed and they arranged to meet up later.

Guy and Jacqui were like chalk and cheese. She was self confident, and breezed through life without a care in the world. She always had a good looking guy in tow, but dispensed with boyfriends like she'd throw away old tights. She was a stunning looking girl and, despite her history of never getting serious with any man, had a queue of them who were interested in her. Even though she was four years younger than her brother, he looked on her as a big sister when it came to someone to turn to.

Guy drove into town and parked the Porsche in the car park at his agent's office. He usually parked there whether or not he was seeing Julian because he thought it was safer than if it was left in a public place. He walked into the town centre and waited for Jacqui outside the main shopping mall. He knew she wouldn't be on time so lit up a cigarette, which he regretted when a Rovers fan saw him and shouted jokingly across the square that it would stunt his growth. To make it worse, Jacqui arrived and saw him stubbing it out. When he blurted out an excuse and made out he only smoked about ten a week, she laughed and told him she wasn't bothered if it was ten an hour.

She led him off to get a coffee saying she needed at least two cups after a heavy night socialising. He quizzed her about finishing with her boyfriend and was amazed at how little it meant to her, even though they'd been together for over six months. By the sound of it, she'd got the next one lined up already. Jacqui asked Guy what he'd got in mind in terms of presents for family and friends, and she either granted her approval of them or dismissed them as out of the question. Where she didn't agree, Guy crossed them off his list and asked what would be better. Jacqui being Jacqui, she quickly suggested something eminently more suitable.

As he expected, Guy was led away to a department store to buy his sister's gift first. She took an expensive designer label dress off a rack and he waited outside the changing rooms as she went in to try it on. Guy jumped when he got a tap on the shoulder. He turned to see Shane Forbes smiling at him. Shane said he'd seen a glimpse of the girl Guy was with before she went to try on her new dress. He said Guy was a dark horse, keeping that from everyone when most of the lads didn't think he'd got a 'regular bird'. Guy wondered what to say and decided against explaining that he was with his sister. He hoped Shane would quickly wander off and no harm would be done. Just then a slim blonde girl joined them holding at least five items, told Shane she wouldn't be long, and walked to the cubicles, looking back to smile at him. Shane gestured that they should sit down while they waited. He joked that Guy was trying to peek through the gap in the curtains, and he asked him how long he'd been going out with this good looking girl. All Guy could think of doing was answering vaguely, saying it wasn't long. He regretted more and more that he'd not said straight away that Jacqui was his younger sister, as he dug himself deeper into a dilemma of his own making. Shane said they should go out as a four sometime soon, and he asked even more questions. Guy, looking anxiously towards the cubicles, tried to change the subject each time and divert the conversation to football and the team. After a few minutes, to Guy's immense relief, the blonde girl, rather than his sister, emerged before dragging his team-mate off to the till to pay for her new clothes. Minutes later, Jacqui emerged wearing the dress. She jokingly pouted and posed and asked her brother's opinion of it. Looking to see that Shane and his partner had left the floor, Guy smiled back and said she looked devastating.

As the two of them went from shop to shop, Guy thought about the episode with Shane. He felt stupid for not being honest. He'd subconsciously thought, when his colleague first appeared, that it might be a quick opportunity to look like his other team-mates. Had Jacqui come out first however, met the waiting Shane and then entered into conversation with him as she surely would, then he would have been in trouble. Jacqui had later explained to him that her ex-boyfriend had rung while she was half-dressed and she had needed to fend off his questions about their split. Much as he sympathised with the man's predicament, he was delighted he'd rung her. Guy also thought, as he had many times before, that it might pay him to get some sort of girlfriend, if only for occasions like these. And just like he'd concluded many times before, he realised it was bad enough living a lie without involving someone else in it all.

• • •

The coach left the Rovers ground in pouring rain. It was Monday morning and the squad were travelling up for their game at Middlesborough the next evening. Recognising the run they were on and listening to their manager, the board had agreed that they would book in at a north Yorkshire hotel where they could train on Monday afternoon and prepare well for their top-of-the-table clash.

Guy had areas of his life where he had a great deal of self-confidence. The minute the whistle blew for a match he would believe he could influence the game and be the best player on the pitch. This didn't often happen, but he knew that, most games, he'd be one of the best - and the very best, a few times a season. Training, to him, was a challenge that he relished every day. The routines may have been fairly predictable; in fact the Rovers coaching staff were some of the least imaginative he'd played under, but the challenge to be the fittest and the most skilful player in the squad still remained, and he loved it. Other parts of his sporting life were the opposite and he suffered from a lack of self-belief in many situations. The social side of being a team player proved difficult for him, and he had no idea how to play a part in the banter that was a constant in a player's life. Little things, like boarding the team bus, were difficult. Knowing where to sit was the problem. Should he join the bulk of the players in the back of the coach and then have to try and contribute to the mickey-taking and tall stories for mile after mile. Or should he sit towards the front on his own, listening to music - and either feel left out or be suspected of being aloof. The one thing that struck Guy when he thought about this part of away trips was that this was something he dwelled on a lot, and it was something that the majority of his fellow players probably never thought about for a single second. They got out of their cars, got on the bus, and got on with it.

Today, Guy compromised. Rovers often took a couple of youth team players with them on away trips so that they could sample the experience of being with the first team. They would be given little tasks, so that they felt like they were contributing. Guy sat next to Stevie, a shy seventeen-year-old full-back, who was travelling with the squad for only the second or third time. He was a quiet lad and Guy knew they'd probably chat politely for maybe only a few minutes, and then settle down to read or listen to their iPods. As it was, they had a conversation for over an hour, despite the din of laughter and horsing around behind them. Guy was impressed with Stevie's plans for his career and was embarrassed to hear that he, Guy, was held up as someone the young man would like to emulate at the club. They agreed to meet up and do extra training together over the next few weeks and they exchanged phone numbers. Then they were interrupted when players at the rear of the coach shouted to their young helper to stop talking and make teas and coffees for them, which he dutifully did.

The squad trained for an hour in the afternoon and then rested in their rooms. Guy shared with Nathan, who played with his portable games console until it was time for the squad to assemble for a team meeting in a function room downstairs. Guy hated staying in a room with another player. He could never understand why clubs, especially those at the highest level, made their players share bedrooms. He would gladly make a donation out of his wages if it meant he could have his own room when the team travelled away. He didn't particularly like Nathan, who was untidy, noisy, and oblivious to the needs of his room-mate. Guy had tried to sleep but couldn't and he knew he probably wouldn't sleep well at night either. After Nathan had left the room, Guy tried to feel better about their arrangement by tidying up and restoring some semblance of order before he joined the rest of the squad for the meeting.

The manager rarely spoke to the team as a whole for any length of time. He preferred instead to speak to each player in turn. As the meeting began, he told them that their match at the Riverside was one of the most important games in the club's history. They were to give everything to try and get a result. He wouldn't tolerate any player who didn't leave the pitch exhausted after ninety minutes As usual, Guy was one of the last to be summoned to speak to Davie Adams.

"Right Guy, you're our out-ball. Make yourself available for the easy pass and I'm relying on you to create something. Whether it's a chance for someone else or you do it on your own, I don't give a fuck. While the others are killing themselves keeping that lot out, you're the one with the brains to grab us a half chance. Understand?" he said. "Yes, Davie, no problem," replied Guy, as he rose from his seat.

"I haven't finished. Sit down. If we're a goal up it's different. You're gonna have to defend. You're gonna have to stop their full-back pushing up. You're good going forward but you're shit at helping your mates. So, for once, prove me wrong. Hurt your fucking self. Tackle. Hit the bastards. Not just wave your foot about at the fucking ball."

"OK, I know what you mean," said Guy, irritated.

"The day you get a card for taking someone out is the day I book an open-top bus," said Davie. "I'd fucking celebrate. Now think about what I've said."

"Will do boss."

"Make sure you do."

At night, Guy tossed and turned and couldn't get to sleep. Nathan was still downstairs and he was clearly breaking the manager's curfew. He was last seen with Shane, hidden in an alcove in one of the smaller bars, talking to two young girls. The manager's comments had upset Guy. He never praised him for all the positive contributions he made, and yet again had criticised him for his lack of strength in defending. Guy reached over and took a gulp of wine. He'd guessed he wouldn't sleep and had riskily acquired a bottle from reception in the hope it would relax him. As he swallowed another mouthful, he wished he'd bought another. Seeing that the bottle was nearly empty, he rang down and did just that.

Guy opened his eyes. He wondered for a second where he was and what the sounds were that had interrupted his sleep. It was dark, but faint gasping sounds and the squeak of moving furniture could be heard from the other side of the room. Confused, Guy's instinct was to remain lying on his side and make out he was still asleep. He looked at the wardrobe on his side of the room and in the mirror on the door he could see the source of the noises. As his eyes became used to the murky light, he could make out Nathan's naked form as he stood thrusting himself at a girl sitting on the dressing table facing him, her legs wrapped around his waist. She was wearing only her shoes and, as the minutes passed by, her gasps became louder and quicker. Guy listened and watched. With nothing else to distract him, the reflection and the noises slowly turned him on. In the thin sliver of light that escaped from the bathroom door, he saw a bead of sweat trickle between Nathan's muscular shoulders, down his spine, and into the small of his back. Just for a second, until he collected his thoughts, he wished it was him there enjoying it.

Still pretending to be asleep, and wishing he could get into a more comfortable position, Guy waited as Nathan and the girl finished having sex. Then they giggled and swore as they fumbled about getting dressed before leaving the room. Guy rose and went to the bathroom for a drink of water. He knew Nathan would soon return and he would have to lie in bed pretending to be asleep again. He thought he'd probably not sleep again until morning. All he could think was that when his playing days were over, he'd never share a room again. Not unless sharing was on his terms, that is.

• • •

It finished 'Boro' 5, Rovers 1. The manager went ballistic. Not one player escaped his wrath. Usually, they wouldn't take much notice because Adams was always angry, but they'd never seen him like this. Rovers had gone one up early on, defended as well as they could – but then, after the equaliser went in, capitulated. Even Frankie, their captain, was on the receiving end. And, of course, Guy got it the most. Adams stood in front of him, his red face barely inches from Guy's, screaming abuse at him. Most of the players thought Guy wouldn't be able to take it, but he did. He just stood there in front of them, listening and expressionless.

Deciding where to sit on the team coach wasn't an issue on the return journey. Nobody would be talking and no one would be messing around. Guy sat near the front of the bus and stared out of the window into the gloom across the windswept car park. He was in shock. He'd played well; he'd set up their goal. But when it came to defending and following the manager's instructions, he'd failed miserably. Guy couldn't understand why he possessed so much pace when he attacked defences with the ball, and yet he couldn't even keep up when he tracked back and followed an overlapping full-back. He didn't understand either why he'd kill himself to dive in, in the opposing penalty area, to get a touch on the ball to score, but he couldn't get a foot in and make a clean tackle on the edge of his own penalty area.

He always felt it was unfair when Adams picked him out and berated him, but tonight he thought he deserved it. And he realised that the way he played football was the way he lived his life. When he was in control and doing things he was good at, he was alive and confident; when he needed to confront things and overcome them, he was a sad, nervous, little mouse. One that hid away, avoided people and problems, and kept secrets. Stevie entered the bus and sat down alongside Guy. As the coach pulled away from the ground, Stevie whispered to Guy that he thought he'd had a good game and it was up to defenders to defend. He said he would look forward to doing some extra training with him. They smiled at each other and then settled down, both to try and sleep their way through the long journey ahead of them.

• • •

The players jogged around the pitch until the coach shouted at them to speed up. The manager stood close by with his arms folded. As expected, Adams had instructed the squad to report for training the next morning; a predictable punishment for losing so heavily the night before. Most of the players knew that they wouldn't be worked hard. The penalty for their abject performance was having to get up and drive to the training ground, instead of having the day to rest. Their penance would also include being criticised and, in some cases, abused, as Adams looked to relieve the pent-up anger he would have felt all night.

As they ran they were told to sprint, jump, turn, and stop for press-ups and sit-ups. To Guy, this was the sort of stuff he'd expect from a Sunday League club and, if the manager and his staff wanted their players to learn from their mistakes, they should analyse them and work on their weaknesses. Because he was active and didn't have to listen, Guy wasn't particularly worried when Adams started on him. He was called a wimp and told to grow some bollocks. He was threatened with being reduced to train with the youth team (which, incidentally, he wouldn't have minded because their coaches were much better) if he didn't learn to help his teammates and defend better. For good measure, Adams finished his rant by telling Guy that if he didn't buck up he would be put up against a wall and fucking thrashed to within an inch of his miserable fucking life. Thankfully, the manager then turned his attention to Aaron, the keeper.

Back at home, Guy lay on the settee. The afternoon and evening ahead of him, he decided he needed to do something positive rather than sit around thinking about his performance at the Riverside Stadium. If he didn't, he would only expand his thoughts to much wider issues and slide into a depression. He would also smoke too many cigarettes and probably drink too much. Whilst it was the main source of his dark moods, he couldn't help thinking how much easier it would be to have someone to talk to about all his problems. Not a parent or any other relative. Not a mate either. Someone close. Someone he could lie with. But if he did, then, for all the talking they could do, the reasons for his pain would be ten times worse.

Just then his mobile rang. Zoe greeted him and told him that their agent had asked if they could stand in last-minute for another band whose singer was ill. She knew that he wasn't allowed to perform with them during the week, but thought she'd ask anyway. Guy told her he'd love to. The gig was in north London and they agreed to meet at around six in order to have plenty of time to get there and set up. Guy was delighted. He'd got the perfect alternative to spending hours on his own. Two or three hours of thrashing out riffs on his guitar in a gloomy basement club would be a complete escape from feeling thoroughly miserable.

Guy often got in the mood for playing with the band by having a few drinks. He wasn't a big drinker, and he knew having too much would impair his guitar playing, but tonight he wasn't too worried about how he performed. He just wanted to get on stage and escape from all the anxiety of football and everything else. He had taken a bottle of vodka with him, and he added it to the soft drinks they were provided with back stage.

The first session was good. The venue was dark and atmospheric. The audience consisted of regular clubbers and what looked like a large group of people who were out celebrating together. They looked like they had been drinking for some time. From the off, Zoe got the band to perform some lively well-known stuff and the punters loved it. The dance floor was soon a mass of energy with people packed together dancing to the deafening music. Guy was completely engrossed in his playing and drenched with sweat. The first set sped by, each song being greeted with cheers. Zoe told the crowd they'd be back in twenty minutes and they left the stage to cries of "More! More!"

Guy went out through a fire door and stood in the small rear yard smoking. He was drunk, wet through, hot, and elated. He turned to go back in and jumped when he saw a slim young man standing there. Guy had noticed him earlier when he was playing. He instinctively found his lighter, leaned over, and lit the cigarette that was hanging from his lips. The man thanked Guy and said his name was Nick. He was celebrating his birthday. He said he'd argued with his partner who had left, and he wasn't going to let that spoil his evening. He said he thought Guy looked great on stage. Then he thanked Guy for the light and asked him if they could have a drink together later. Guy told him that would be OK. Nick smiled and went back into the building.

The second set was even more explosive that the first. Guy drank between numbers but he was so high with the occasion he knew that, for once, being drunk didn't matter. The dancers wouldn't let them stop and they played until they couldn't physically play any more. Zoe's voice gave up, and they were all exhausted when they staggered away from the stage. The minute Guy stepped down on to the dance floor, Nick was there. He held Guy's arm firmly, led him from the building, and took him straight to a waiting taxi.

The sound of letters falling through the letterbox woke Guy up. He was lying on the settee in his flat. He blinked and immediately his head filled with a combination of questions and hazy memories of the night before. The man he'd met had directed the cab to his house in Crouch End. He had straddled Guy on the back seat of the taxi as soon as it drove away from the club. He remembered the taxi driver had said "For fuck's sake" when he saw them kissing in the rear view mirror. Guy knew that they had had sex on the floor at Nick's house. He hadn't a clue how he got home. Apart from feeling anxious about leaving his guitar behind at the club, and hoping Zoe would have looked after it, Guy felt exhilarated that he had met someone. The impulsive nature of their meeting only added to him feeling good. For months he'd lived a routine where time to think was his enemy. Such time had made him convinced he shouldn't do things he really wanted to. He hadn't had time for a single thought when the band built the crowd into a near-frenzy, and he'd hadn't had a second to question a single thing when he had been seduced. He'd just let it happen and he'd enjoyed every moment.

• • •

Guy spent the rest of the week with the events of Wednesday night on his mind. He was sure he'd given Nick his phone number, and he was equally sure their attraction for each other would mean that they would meet up again and things would develop. He wasn't too concerned that he hadn't heard from him by Saturday and he was far from concerned when he got to the ground and was told he would be on the bench for their home game with Preston. He'd realised that there was more to life than just football and, whilst he knew he'd still have to keep secrets, he felt more sure than ever he could balance everything successfully. He was pleased to have the pressure of being in the starting eleven taken off him. He knew that if he was brought on it would be to chase the game and not help hold on to a lead.

In the end, that's pretty much how it turned out. Two down, Rovers pulled a goal back when the Preston centre-half pulled down Scott Hobbs as he burst into the box. The red card was shown and the penalty converted. With fifteen minutes to go, Guy went on and with his first few touches beat the full-back and crossed for Kadojo to volley home. Guy also hit a volley from twenty yards that clipped the top of the bar and Rovers heaped on the pressure, but the winner wouldn't come. Again, they'd got a point from a game they looked like losing – and, again, they'd got a point that kept them up near the promotion places.

Guy was pleased with his contribution. He wondered as he changed if being a bit-part player might suit him more than being a regular in the team. If not much was expected of him, then maybe his contributions would seem more significant. He'd also be under less pressure. When he started a game he always felt like he'd got to be a world-beater. Anyway, he thought he'd feel good about the game for the next few days, just like he still felt pretty good about other things. Adams went around the dressing room speaking to each player. He said to Guy "about fucking time", which pleased him. That was the nearest he'd ever had to praise from his manager.

• • •

Guy visited his mother on Sunday, and was pleased to hear that Jacqui was coming round to join them for lunch. Guy's mother and father had divorced when he was five years old. Even at that tender age, he could tell that his father treated her badly, however much she tried to hide it. Since then, Guy's contact with his dad had been minimal and their meetings had always been strained. He spoke to his mother nearly every day and knew that, if he didn't earn so much and own his trendy flat, he'd probably still be living with her in the family home.

During lunch, Jacqui told them about a trip to Seattle she'd been on for her PR company and described a guy she'd met at a wedding, although it wasn't clear if he was now her latest official boyfriend. Guy described his football appearances and the midweek gig he did, although he missed out details of the events after it. Nick hadn't rung and, by now, he was wondering if he'd been the subject of a one-night stand. After all, he had said that he'd got a partner and, despite Guy thinking that the relationship might be over, it may be that they'd made up. At any rate, Guy would never tell his mother that he had met someone. He thought she suspected, if not knew, he was gay, but it was something they never discussed.

Guy told them about the players' Christmas party that was taking place in a couple of days. He said he wasn't keen to go because he hadn't got anyone to take, but missing it was a worse option, such would be the merciless stick that anyone absent would get. Jacqui, true to form, told him to buck up and grab the situation by the throat. Either get someone stunning to accompany him, or be strong about being there on his own. Don't just wimp about making excuses, she said. She then leaned across and whispered in his ear, describing something a work colleague did in similar circumstances last year. She said it went down a storm and it would if Guy did the same. She insisted he did it, and Guy, smiling, said maybe he would.

As he drove away from his mother's house, the phone bleeped to tell him he'd got a text. Guy didn't recognise the number and read it as he drove. The sender thanked him for the other night and said they might meet up again sometime. Guy felt pleased that Nick had at last got in touch and thought that, even though the message didn't definitely suggest another date, maybe, for once, things were going well. He thought his sister's idea for dealing with the players' evening was a good one. He decided he'd damn well go for it.

• • •

In the taxi to the party Guy nervously looked at the package on the seat next to him. He arrived at the hotel and went into the gents' toilets, where he opened the box and emptied its contents. Walking though reception, the hotel staff gasped. He smiled and told them it was "just his little joke". He went through the dining room and walked across to his team-mates and their wives and girlfriends who were already assembled in the bar area. As they saw him, the hum of conversation stopped and, instead of the peals of laughter he anticipated, the room became silent. Guy saw some of the women turn their back on him, and he heard the word "disgusting" uttered by one of them. Frankie asked him what the hell he was playing at. Guy's confidence that bringing a blow-up sex doll to the function as a jokey alternative to bringing a partner was fading by the second. Jacqui had told him her workmate's entrance in that way had been met with riotous laughter and applause. So far, the only laughter Guy had caused was sniggering from the youth team players in one corner and that seemed to be at his expense not because they enjoyed the joke. Slowly, the players and their partners started to divert their attention from him to each other again, and Guy was clearly excluded from their conversations. He knew that some of the hushed voices were talking about him, as one individual or another glanced accusingly over their shoulder in his direction. He wished a huge void would appear in the carpeted floor and he could fall into it. Not knowing what on earth to do as he stood there with the plastic figure under his arm, he went back into the dining area and propped it on to the seat marked "Guy's Guest", alongside his own place. Then he returned to the bar, bought a large vodka and tonic and stood on his own, his heart still pounding with embarrassment.

After a few minutes, which to Guy seemed to last an age, a member of staff announced that dinner was about to be served. Bitterly regretting his decision to place the doll at his table, Guy walked slowly over and joined the others, most of whom had already taken their seats. As he sat down, Aaron suggested that it was best that he got rid of the object next to him. This was advice Guy hardly needed and, panicking and fumbling, he'd already started to look for the valve to deflate it. As he squeezed it, the expelled air made a high pitched whining sound, and Guy's face went redder than ever. One of the girls said he ought to give it a prick, which made some of them snigger. Another, to loud laughter from the rest of them, said Guy wouldn't know how to use his on something like that. By now Guy was sweating and shaking. As soon as he was able to, he pushed the deflated figure under the table, sat down and drank a full glass of wine in one go.

As the first course arrived, the attention gradually turned away from Guy, and the players and partners talked and laughed amongst themselves. To regain some semblance of composure, Guy tried to talk to Scott to his left and to Adele, Shane's pregnant girlfriend, to his right. Adele was polite but no more. When Guy told Scott he'd only brought his artificial guest to be funny, he was told abruptly that it hadn't worked and, if he was the sort who couldn't bring a girl like everyone else, he should have stayed away. Guy, stunned, couldn't understand why his joke, albeit maybe not such a funny one, had met with such hostility. As the dinner went on, he didn't have the courage to say another word to anyone.

As soon as the main course was served, Guy ate a couple of mouthfuls, put his knife and fork together, stood up, and went to the bar. He bought a double vodka, drank it, and ordered another. Fidgeting and feeling horrendously awkward, he checked his phone, if only to occupy his shaking hands. He saw he'd had a text from Stevie. It told him to meet him in the car park around the back of the building at half-past-nine. Guy looked at his watch. It was nine thirty-five. He swallowed his drink and walked quickly out of the building.

The cold night air made Guy shiver and he felt drunk. He tripped on a kerb as he walked around the car park looking for Stevie. Eventually, he heard a voice beckoning him. Stevie told him he'd only got a minute and he didn't want his mates to find out what he was doing. He asked Guy if he'd read any of the message boards on the fan's websites. Guy said he never bothered reading them. Stevie told him that, in the last twenty-four hours or so, they'd been rife with stories about him. He said a director's son was claiming that his boyfriend had cheated on him by going off with one of Rovers' players and sleeping with him. He was saying the player was promiscuous and preyed on younger men. He was determined to get him the sack. Stevie said that the boy was a spoilt rich kid and he wanted the manager to be disciplined too. Rumour had it that his father was trying to keep things quiet but, like any club anywhere, secrets could never be kept. Lots of fans now knew all about it and that the player concerned was him. Because things like this spread like wildfire, the players all knew too. Stevie then said that, whatever Guy might say in the future, they hadn't had this conversation, and that he needed to get back to his pals. He then turned and ran back towards the hotel.

Guy stepped backwards and leaned on a wall. He felt nauseous and cold, but he was covered in sweat. All he could think of doing was getting away. To his horror, he realised that the keys to his flat were in his coat pocket, which he had left in reception when he arrived earlier. Staying in the shadows, he walked around the car park so that he could see the reception area through a window. He crept closer for a better view and tripped over the edge of a path, grazing his knee and tearing his trousers. From there, it looked like there were only staff in the foyer, so Guy took a deep breath, walked up the steps, opened the front door and went in.

As soon as he approached the reception desk, he looked across and was shocked to see Lee, Frankie, Nathan and their partners sitting around a coffee table in a secluded alcove. It looked like they were sharing bottles of champagne.
"Hey up, it's Guy. Just in time mate, there's a telephone call for you!" shouted Nathan, standing and lifting his mobile phone high above his head.
"Who's that calling Guy then, Nathan?" asked Frankie, very deliberately.
"It's Darren," he replied loudly.
Guy tried to ignore them, and hoped the girl at the desk would find his coat as quickly as possible.
"Darren who?" asked Frankie, even more deliberately and at the top of his voice.
"Darren… BENT!" shouted Nathan, and the six of them roared with laughter.
Guy grabbed his coat and, shaking, turned to leave. As he left the building he bumped into Davie Adams, who had told the squad he'd be joining them during the evening. By now, Guy was so upset he could hardly speak.
"Don't come to training tomorrow," said Adams. "See me in my office afterwards. One o'clock."

Guy lit a cigarette and looked across the courtyard. It was late and it was very cold but he didn't feel it as he chain-smoked and gulped vodka on the balcony. A pretty blonde girl wearing a white bath robe walked out on to the balcony next to his and looked across at him. He automatically hid the cigarette down by his side. He heard a male voice through the french doors behind her; she smiled at him, turned and went back in. Guy's mind was racing with worry. As soon as he arrived back at the flat he'd logged on to the supporters' website and read the vile contributions. He'd turned the laptop off after reading only a fraction of the postings about him. Because he was a good player, but not a hard one, he'd been always appreciated by the home fans, but he'd never been a real favourite. He couldn't imagine the reaction he'd get from them now. The opposition fans would be ten times worse. And the opposing players would be a hundred times worse than that. That's if he ever played again. He thought about how his team-mates had been with him earlier in the evening. Were they really that prejudiced? Or was their vitriol down to him letting them and the club as a whole down when they were doing well and needed to pull together? He wished, as he had a million times during his career, that others before him had pioneered this situation so that he didn't have to, or so that the impact now wouldn't be so great. But no one had. It was down to him. If he'd been a better guitar player than footballer, no one would bat an eyelid. But he wasn't and he would now pay for being a part of one of the only professions that couldn't deal with it, either when it was a secret or when it was known by everyone.

Much later, drunk and cold, Guy crawled into bed still fully clothed. He eventually drifted into a shallow sleep but woke minutes later. As he'd sank into semi-consciousness, all he could see was Adams' huge, purple face grotesquely contorted, inches from his, screaming obscenities at him, covering him in spittle. One by one, all the Rovers' players had appeared behind their manager, screaming at him too. Guy remained awake until dawn, terrified of the day ahead.

• • •

It was a bright cold morning. On the heath, people walked quickly to work or slowly with their dogs. Guy ran through the trees maintaining a good pace. A young mum, pushing her little girl in a pushchair, looked surprised as he ran towards her. On being asked, he stopped to sign an autograph for her. He smiled when she said all her family were Rovers fans. Guy set off again, vowing to spend the morning working on his fitness. He was going to complete a six mile run and then do some shuttles. He might be missing training at the club, but that didn't mean he had to sit around doing nothing.

Earlier, Guy had shaved, drunk half a carton of orange juice and thrown his remaining cigarettes in the bin. He had then retrieved them, put them under the tap and soaked them in water, before throwing them away again. He decided to spend the morning wisely before going to the ground. At one stage last night, he had fleetingly thought that jumping from the balcony would solve everything. The thought lasted a second and he soon knew that such an action was stupid, selfish, and unnecessary. Nevertheless he'd thought about it. He was still scared and he was still deeply hurt. There was lots of things to resolve but now he'd decided he'd meet things head on and be strong. As strong as he could be, at least.

Some schoolboys were the next to recognise him, and they were delighted when he joined in with their kick-about. Guy dribbled round them as they tried to get the ball, and he played a one-two off a waste bin before rolling the ball under the boy in goal and between the two school bags that acted as goal posts. He stayed and chatted to them for a few minutes before resuming his run. He ran alongside the canal and thought about his career. He would probably be told later that he had no place at the club any more. Football being football, word would spread and no other club would take him on. He wasn't a criminal, he hadn't done anything wrong, but he would be an outcast.

After the shuttles, some squat thrusts and push ups, Guy jogged home. He rang his mother and said he might stay with her for a few days. She said she'd be delighted if he did. He showered and walked through to the kitchen drying himself. Looking around, he decided he'd put the flat on the market straight away. He dressed, left the building, and drove to the ground.

The changing rooms were deserted. As usual, the players had quickly departed after training. Guy walked along the corridor and was grateful he was on his own. He looked into the home dressing room and realised that, if he wasn't going to be transferred, things wouldn't be the same in there again. If the club wanted him to leave then nothing would be the same again. He turned and was startled to see Frankie Thomas standing facing to him.

"I've waited for you, "said Frankie, "I know you're meeting the gaffer at one."
"Yes, I'm not looking forward to it," said Guy.
"I don't blame you. You know he thumped the chairman at Athletic just before he came here, don't you?"
"God, did he?"
"They didn't want him to leave. The chairman tried every dodgy trick in the book to put Rovers off. Davie sorted it the only way he knows how."
"Christ," said Guy, more nervous than ever.
"Look Guy, I can't pretend that I've liked you while you've been here," said Frankie "You've never been one of the lads. Sorry. I didn't mean that how it sounded."
"That's OK."
"You've never hung around with us. Always pissing about with that band of yours. And you've never been one for a laugh and a joke. But as captain, I want you to know that me and the lads will support you. If the gaffer isn't kicking you out, that is. I just wanted to let you know that before you meet him. You'll get grief from people in this club, and god knows what from outside it. Probably too much to bear. But you're part of our team. We just wanted you to know that."
"Thanks. I appreciate that. Has he spoken to you?" asked Guy.
"No," replied Frankie. "He normally has a word with me about team things. But not this. He's probably too angry. You better get in there. It's gone one o'clock."

Guy shook hands with his captain and walked along to the manager's office. He was terrified and his hands shook as he knocked and turned the door handle to enter. He'd heard Adams' raised voice as he approached the office. Adams stood near the window holding his mobile phone to his ear as Guy entered; he abruptly gestured to him to sit down.

"Look Jim, I rely on you to make the chairman see sense. I can't speak to the fucking bloke. You're vice-chairman and I need you to tell him what I'm doing. He doesn't know a fucking thing about football. He's a prat. All he can talk about is 'blue sky thinking' and all that shit. Management-speak that means fuck all. You've got to sort it out. I need a fucking decision!"

By now, Guy was in a state of panic. Was this conversation about him? Surely they had sorted out what they were going to do before this meeting. He contemplated running out of the office if the opportunity arose.

"Oh, for fuck's sake, man! You're useless! I'll sort it out my fucking self!" shouted Adams, and he closed the phone and threw it down on to the desk. He sat down, facing his player. His face was red with anger from his previous conversation. He waited a few seconds before addressing Guy.

"Have you met Irene?" he said.

"Er... what?"asked Guy.

"Irene, my wife. Have you met her?"

"Er, no, I haven't. Sorry."

"She wants you to come for lunch on Sunday."

" Sorry?" said Guy, completely nonplussed.

"Are you deaf lad? Lunch on Sunday. Look son, I've always been hard on you. That's 'cos you're our best player. If I'm hard on you, you try harder. Makes you a better player."

"Right," said Guy, confused, but breathing a little easier.

"My job is to get results. End of," said Adams. "I have to be heavy with you and get you to win us games. I'm not paid to worry about your feelings. That's why I've always given you stick."

"I've never minded," said Guy "Not usually."

"We'll get through this. You're a good lad."

"I don't know what to say."

"You don't need to say anything," said Adams.

"Wasn't that about me ? That argument."
"Hell, no. That was about increasing my budget. The squad's too thin. Like I say lad, we'll get through this. You'll get untold grief. But I'll help you. I'm not letting them ruin your career. I'll sort it out with the directors. You just concentrate on playing football. Ignore everything else."
"Thanks boss, I thought I'd be sold. Or sacked. I thought I'd never play again."
"You know Jimmy? The kit man."
"Yes," replied Guy.
"He's a poof. Sorry. He's gay," said Adams "He thinks no one knows. I do. I know everything at this club. At least I do now."
"I thought you'd want me out."
"Let me tell you something. We've got one lad, me and Irene. Lives in Germany now. Only started speaking to me again a year ago. He had problems. Drug problems. I was too engrossed in football to notice. I never spent any time with him. He was terrified I'd find out - and when I did, I hammered him. He was a fool for getting into it, but he did. And I made it worse. I was a pig-headed fool. He didn't need me to hurt him. He'd done enough of that to himself."
"I'm sorry," said Guy, "that must have been hard."
"I lost my son. For a long time." said Adams "His mother did too, because of me. I'll never get him back, not properly. Not like when he was a youngster. I'm not losing you as a player. We'll get through it. Off you go. Training tomorrow. Three points on Saturday."
"Thanks boss," said Guy, as he rose and walked to the door.
"And don't forget Sunday," said Adams.

In the car park, Guy breathed in the sharp, cold air. He unlocked the car and sat looking across at the towering main stand. It was deathly quiet now and, in the weeks to come, the noise coming from it would be deafening. Getting promotion would be the big challenge. The biggest challenge in the club's history. And there would be other challenges too. Guy started the engine and drove off, waving to the man on the gate as he drove past.

WILL POWER

As Peter Trevis approached them, Sam stopped work and started to roll a cigarette. Nigel wiped his hands on his overalls in readiness to shake hands with him. Nigel and Sam had been working at the Trevis's property for nearly three weeks now. They were getting used to him strolling down from the house on the pretext of having a friendly chat, when his real motive was to check how they were getting on.

"It looks good gentlemen," said Trevis, although in truth 'it' hadn't changed much from his last inspection a couple of hours earlier.
"Thank you, yes, we're pleased with it," said Nigel, "it's good planting weather at the moment. Neither too dry or too wet."
"Is Doreen looking after you? Tea and all that."
"Yes, very kind. We've set out the new terrace round the corner, if you want to have a look."
"Oh, champion. Yes, let's," said their client, enthused by the news.
The three of them walked around the newly planted area towards a high brick wall, the other side of which stood a large Victorian greenhouse. An area of removed turf and marker posts showed the extent of the new terrace.
"Oh no, that won't do at all," said an alarmed Trevis. "Far too large. My god. It'll look hideous."
"Oh, right," said Nigel, as Sam sighed almost audibly behind them. "Well, we'll change it of course. Smaller if you wish. Not a problem."
"Damn good job I was still here before you'd got much further."
"I suppose so, yes. Sorry about that. We'll reduce it by, say, two feet on these three sides; replace the turf. Will that be OK?"
"Better, yes. Knock on the door when you've done that and you've put down the sand base. We'll have a good idea if you've got it right by then. Right, I'm off. Things to do," and he walked briskly back to the house.
Nigel turned to Sam and said "OK, we'll finish the planting and get on with changing this. Better have it done before we leave, so he's not mulling over it tonight."
"You never cease to amaze me, boss," replied Sam. "The bloody bloke's OK'd your plans, we've done it exactly as they show it, and you let him slag us off when its him who's wrong."
"I don't mind. It's no trouble changing it. I want him to be happy with it all."
"Just 'cos he's a bloody toff doesn't mean you can't stand up to him."
"It's not that," said Nigel. "It's better to change things than have an argument."
"You're too bloody soft," said Sam, flicking the end of his roll-up into a flower bed.

Nigel dropped Sam off after work and he parked the truck in the yard alongside the cottage. Di, his wife, greeted him in the kitchen, and he told her about the work they'd done and what he'd got planned for tomorrow. She made them tea and they discussed their meeting at the solicitor's on Friday. Then the subject of City's match cropped up.

"Are you going to go tonight?" she asked. "I know it'll be emotional for you, but you should start going again."

Surprising her, Nigel said "Yes, I'm going. It'll be OK. I know everyone there, and it'll be nice to see them. I'm going up for a shower, and I'll drop you at your mum's on the way there if you like."

"That's fine love," she replied, pleased at his answer.

It was now three weeks since Nigel's father had died and things, for him, were getting back to some semblance of order. The funeral had taken place, and he had done everything he could to help his mother. His dad had had cancer for a while but Nigel had seen him fade away over a short period of time, almost as if he was ready to go. On the night he died, Nigel sat with him, and he was pleased that he'd gone peacefully and painlessly. His mother's reaction, on the other hand, had shocked him. She must have known they hadn't got long left together and she would surely grieve, but she seemed totally unprepared for his death. After he'd gone, she sat rocking backwards and forwards in a chair downstairs saying "oh dear, oh dear" repeatedly, in a quivering voice for over two hours. She did this on and off until the funeral. The last three weeks had proved that she was going to be dependant on Nigel in many ways. She needed him there as much as possible. He had slept at the house for the first two weeks so that she was not there on her own at night. Every day since then he rang her several times and called in at least once. Di had helped too, by fetching her groceries and cleaning and tidying. Sadly for Nigel, his wife and mother could never really get on, not since the fall-out they had had some years ago. At least Di was helping in ways she felt she could let herself at this difficult time. The one passion Nigel and his father shared was the local football club. His dad had taken him from the age of five when they stood on the open 'popular' side, and, in later years, they both had season tickets together in the main stand. Nigel had missed City's last home game but decided he wasn't going to miss the match tonight against league leaders Charlton, even if the seat next to him would be empty.

City were having a decent season. After a year in League 2, they had been promoted twice in succession, but the standard in the Championship was too much for them. They kicked off in August in League 1, a division, or its equivalent, they had spent most of their history in. Whilst they hadn't put together a run of unbeaten games, they kept picking up points here and there, and Nigel felt a top-ten finish wouldn't be too bad an outcome. He took his seat in the stand and a lot of familiar faces around him greeted him and said they were sorry his father had passed away. In the programme on the supporters trust page, the writer mentioned his dad's death and paid a nice tribute to his support of the club and his enthusiasm in joining the trust. A flustered young man sitting on the same row slid towards Nigel and asked if it was OK to sit on his father's seat. A decent crowd had turned up to see Charlton and there was a fair bit of confusion with latecomers struggling to find seats, so Nigel smiled and said it was fine. In a way, he felt less uncomfortable.

At around twenty to eight, the players came out on to the pitch and over to his right, Nigel noticed the directors and guests take their seats. City's chairman Bill Spence, however, continued along the gangway and made his way towards Nigel. He shook hands with him and said how sorry he was to hear of his father's death. Slightly stunned, Nigel thanked him and Spence smiled and went back to the directors box. He was well known for his gruffness and wasn't one to spend much time honing his skills at communicating to the club's fans, so Nigel felt quite moved by this brief display of kindness.

The game was a cracker. Both keepers were busy and there were chances at either end. There were no goals until full-time approached. Then Charlton took the lead and City equalised within a minute. As Nigel left the ground, everyone agreed with him it was a fair result.

Next morning, working at the Trevis's, Nigel told Sam about the club chairman making the effort to come and see him. Never one to beat about the bush, Sam said, "He bloody well should do, the money you and your dad have spent following that lot."

Sam had worked for Nigel's landscaping business for nearly three years. He was a good worker and, having started as a labourer, was now good at identifying plants and being left to construct landscaping features such as patios, planters, and pergolas. It was now October, so business was less hectic, but they still had maintenance jobs to do as well, as a waiting list of garden designs to come up with and carry out on site. The only issue was Sam's diplomacy, or lack of it, and Nigel often had to divert him away from a customer to avoid any problems. This particular morning, Sam decided to approach the subject of Nigel's wife and mother.

"Your missus gonna bury the hatchet with your mum then, now your dad's dead?" he asked.

"Not as easy as that Sam."

"She was out of order you know. Bloody telling you Di was playing away from home with me. When we weren't. Bloody hell. Bit much that."

"Look, Sam," said Nigel, "my mum was wrong. She's always been a gossip merchant and she went too far. It really hurt Di that did. Lasting damage and all that. Give her time."

"Only brought it up 'cos you're knackered looking after your ma. Be much easier if Di forgave her and gave you a hand."

"I know, mate. Di's the best thing that ever happened to me - but she's proud. When dad died the first thing she said was 'don't you think your mother is going to live with us'. That's how much she holds a grudge about it. I don't blame her but I'm caught in the middle," said Nigel.

"OK mate. Fair enough," said Sam and, seeing Trevis in the distance, added. "Look out, Bertie-Big-Bollocks is on the prowl again. Heads down."

• • •

On Friday morning Nigel did a couple of hours work with Sam before leaving him with instructions about the jobs he wanted him to get done. He then drove home to shower and get changed. His mother lived a couple of miles away and she was ready and dressed to the nines for their meeting with her solicitor. This was clearly going to be an ordeal for her and Nigel felt great warmth towards her as she stood at the front door waiting for him to arrive. At the solicitors, they were shown straight in to see Mr Forsythe, who had dealt with the Day family's legal matters for over twenty years.

"Good morning, Mrs Day, good morning, Nigel. Can I just say how sorry I am to be seeing you under these circumstances. Can I get you a cup of tea?" he asked. He went on to explain that much of what he had to talk about was routine but necessary under these sort of circumstances, and he would keep it as brief as possible. He explained how the house deeds, Mr Day's pension, shares, savings accounts and so on would be put in Mrs Day's name because, naturally, his will had confirmed so. There would be some papers for her to sign to complete these arrangements. Nigel was never particularly aware of his father's financial standing, but since he had retired, it seemed his parents were reasonably comfortable.
"There is, however, one final element of Mr Day's will that is, shall I say, slightly unorthodox," said Mr Forsythe earnestly. "Nigel, your father wished to thank you for the many happy years you spent together watching the local football team. His will recognises this. In short, we were instructed to approach the board of directors prior to this meeting, which we have done. The sum of £50,000 has been invested in equity at the club and the board have already approved your position in the boardroom. Congratulations Nigel, you are now a director of the football club you so fervently support."
"My god," said Nigel, stunned. "Isn't this money that should have gone to mum?"
"Don't be silly," she butted in, "I've got more than I need. Enjoy it."
"My god," said Nigel again, which was all he could think of saying.

For the next few days, Nigel was both elated and apprehensive. Whilst he was busy with work and visiting his mother, his thoughts were on his new role at the club. He didn't know whether to contact the chairman or the chief executive or wait to see if they would contact him first. City were away at Walsall the day after he was given the news and, whilst he didn't often go to away matches, he wasn't sure if he should go, and what the arrangements would be if he did. In the event, he decided to work instead and was pleased they won 1-0.

Eventually, on Tuesday morning, he got a telephone call from Simon Wall, the club secretary.

"Hi, Nigel, I'm ringing to let you know about the board meeting tomorrow," he said.

"Tomorrow?" queried Nigel. He was taken aback by the short notice of what would be, to him, a momentous event.

"Yep, two in the afternoon. Should last a couple of hours and then you all go for drinks. Because you're new you'll be expected to be there for the duration. Hope that's OK."

"Well, yes, I suppose so," replied Nigel. "Will there be any papers in advance of the meeting for me to read up on?"

"Papers?" said Simon. "Not really. Probably be some on the day. Accounts and all that, maybe. Come up to Neville's office at quarter to two and he'll fill you in with anything you need to know."

Nigel was surprised by the conversation. He wasn't particularly familiar with the workings of a large limited company, but he'd been on the parish council for a few years. He knew that it was usual for an agenda and reports, accounts and so on to be distributed in advance of a meeting to help the decision-making process. And only being told about the meeting the day before didn't help when it came to re-arranging work he'd got planned for him and Sam. Never mind, he thought. This must be the way they work, and a reflection of the pressure they are under. It would be up to him to make a valuable contribution under the same circumstances. He decided as suggested by Simon, he'd see Neville Walker, the chief executive, for half an hour or so before the meeting and ask some questions.

Next morning, Nigel instructed Sam on what work he expected him to do that day. He parried the comments he got back in return about him 'swanning off to the bloody football club' and leaving him 'to deal with that knobhead Trevis.' He drove into town to get some gravel and drop an estimate in at a customer's house just round the corner from his own cottage. Back at home, he washed and changed into a suit, shirt and tie.

Nigel arrived at the ground just before half past one and went into reception. He said he was there to see Mr Walker and a surly young woman, without looking up, told him to go up the stairs and turn left. He knocked and entered the chief executive's office but it was empty. As there were no seats in the corridor outside, he sat down in the office and waited. Five minutes turned into ten and then fifteen. Without wanting to snoop, Nigel glanced at the paperwork strewn almost chaotically across the desk in front of him. Amongst papers labelled 'sponsors' agreements' and so on, he couldn't fail to notice a document bearing the County Court insignia which, although he was reading it upside down, appeared to tell the club they were having legal action taken against them. Another letter, its letterhead obscured, seemed to be telling them steps were being considered for non-payment of previous invoices. Just then loud peals of laughter echoed along the corridor, and Neville and Simon walked in.

"Oh I say, we've got a visitor," said Neville. "Nigel, is it?"

"Yes, I'm very pleased to meet you," replied Nigel anxiously. "Look it's ten to two and I don't mean to be rude, but I'd hoped we'd have a chat before I go into the meeting. Is that OK?"

"'Course it is, old chap, but if you don't mind I'm just going to have to nip down to the little boy's room. We've been with a sponsor for lunch and he would insist I try the guest bitter. Hang on a mo." With that, Neville left the room. Simon smiled and, sensing Nigel was on edge, tried to re-assure him.

"You'll be OK, just go with the flow. The chairman does all the talking anyway. Just one word of warning before you go in," he said. "Mr Spence has been putting pressure on two of the directors, and it's come to a bit of a head this morning. He's told them they need to up their investment in the club or they're off the board. They each put in a few quid a long time ago and have lived off it ever since. Might be a bit of an atmosphere, but don't worry."

"Oh....right," said Nigel, feeling worse by the minute.

Simon showed Nigel to the boardroom and Neville, whistling loudly, walked along the corridor towards them and followed them in. The room was surprisingly small and was dominated by an oval table, a panelled bar in one corner, and a huge painting of a youthful looking Bill Spence on one wall. Men were already sitting around the table and Nigel sat in the only available chair. He nodded to the person sitting opposite him who either didn't notice his greeting or decided to ignore it.

"Right gentlemen, we'll proceed." said Mr Spence. "You'll notice we have a new director with us. Allow me to introduce you to him. This is Nigel Bray who …"

"Er… "Day"," said Nigel.

"What? Oh yes, Day, everyone. Nigel Day. Sadly Nigel's father passed away but, without being too mercenary, his loss is our gain. Nice lump of money put in the club. Nigel has a garden centre in town..."

"Landscape gardener, I'm a landscape gardener," stuttered Nigel.

"Yes, that's what I said. Gardener, yes. Of course. Now I'll invite my colleagues to introduce themselves, starting with my vice-chair," and Spence gestured to his left.

Working clockwise around the table, Nigel was greeted by Fred Goodwin, the vice-chair, Rick Knight, the trust representative, Neville and Simon again, and Alfred Booth and Jake Keys, who, from their general demeanour and muttered greetings, were clearly the disgruntled men described earlier. Nigel noticed there was no agenda and, unless one of the staff was going to bring some documents and distribute them, there were no supporting papers either.

"I'll give you my report, and then we'll get the manager in," said Spence, clearing his throat. "Well, obviously we're doing OK. The team's doing fine. Couple of wins in the next three games and we'll be in the top ten. The overdraft stands at about one and a half, bit more than normal, and the bank are whingeing a bit, but you can leave that to me. Can't they Neville?"

"Of course chairman," replied his chief executive, smiling.

"The gates are down by about 10% but then again we're a division lower this year. I've spoken to the manager and the two highly paid wasters we spoke about last time who he never picks will probably accept a pay-off, if the bank will agree. We'll pay their net wages and we'll save on PAYE and NI. Commercial income isn't bad, most of the boxes have been sold, over half of them anyway, and even though the shop got flooded, it's doing OK. Bar and catering, lotteries, all that stuff is OK. Neville will confirm that. Yes, Knight, you've had your hand up for the last few minutes?"

"Mr Spence, as I've said before, I can't possibly report back to my members, your supporters, on the basis of what you've just said," said Rick. "I'm an accountant. I know what I'm talking about. We need accounts. Profit and loss. Month-by-month accounts. A yearly forecast…"

"Well we can't afford in-house accountants. If you're an accountant you can do it," replied Mr Spence. "And anyway you're not supposed to reveal confidential information."

"I never get any confidential information. Just your summary."

"Well it's about time you and your bloody trust stopped bellyaching and did some fundraising. I gave you a position in here and since then you've raised nothing for this club, while we struggle on."

Rick sat back in his chair and sighed. Nigel tried not to appear as shocked as he felt inside.

"If you want to do something useful," said Mr Spence to Rick, "you can take Nigel here to the Customs and Excise. They're getting very stroppy and you can introduce our new director. Tell them he's looking at bringing in even more investment. Get them off our backs."

Just then there was a knock at the door, and the manager looked around it into the room.

"OK to come in now, chairman?" he asked.

"Of course, Steve," said Spence. "Come in. What have you got to tell us?"

The manager, Steve Ford, had been with the club for five years and for all that time the fans had loved him. He would bring in unknown players and they would blossom. They had done well for a small club and had punched above their weight. He began his report by describing the performances and long-term injuries, and he told them he was thinking of picking a member of the youth squad to make his debut for the first team. As he spoke, Nigel noticed that directors around the table who, apart from Rick, had remained impassive and almost uninterested during the chairman's report, had become responsive and almost animated.

They enthusiastically asked him questions and complimented him on the season so far. Then Ford asked:

"I need to push on, chairman. We can make the play-offs this year. I know of a young striker I can get in on loan from Tottenham, and we'll only have to pay half his wages. They'll pay the rest. How are the finances? Any better?"

"Oh yes, fine," said Spence. Nigel nearly choked on the water he had just started to sip. "Higher up the league means more through the

turnstiles. Leave it with me. Is that OK with you gentlemen?"
Around the table, the directors nodded and replied positively - despite having no idea what the player's earnings were that they had just agreed to pay half of.
"And you haven't told me about my new coach," said the manager. "He's ready to start."
"I've resolved that," said Neville, smiling at his chairman. "He'll be called 'Head Of Youth Development'. His salary will be covered by the League money we get for the Centre of Excellence, but he'll really be your coach. Is that OK?"
"How you do it is up to you. But thanks, that's great," said Ford.

After a break for coffee the meeting resumed and Neville spoke at length. Most of what he told them revolved around general club housekeeping, saving money, avoiding paying bills, cost cutting, and getting new cash in from any source possible, whether ethically or otherwise. When Nigel heard Neville say, jokingly, "If ain't nailed down sell it, and if it is, sponsor it," he knew that this little expression would stay with him for a very long time.

The meeting drew to a close, although even this, like much of the afternoon, wasn't clear to Nigel. The chairman and his vice-chair discussed their arrangements for a golfing weekend. At the same, time Neville told Alfred and Jake he wanted to get rid of the stadium manager because his salary and bonus were too high. Just then, the phone on the bar rang and Simon answered it.
"Taxi's here gentlemen," he said.
"Excellent," said Spence. "Off we go."
Again Nigel wondered what was happening, and while his colleagues put on their jackets and made to leave, he checked his phone. He'd put it on silent and he'd had three missed calls from his mother. Normally he'd ring straight back, but he ran the risk of being left behind, so decided to ring her later. The eight men filed out of the building and climbed into a people-carrier. Less than ten minutes later, they got out and entered the Regent Hotel in the city centre. They walked into a small bar area and Spence ordered a bottle of red wine. Nigel didn't know who this was for so asked the barman for a tonic water and asked Simon next to him what he wanted to drink.

"Cheers, Nigel, I'll have a scotch. By the way, put your money away, this is on the club," replied Simon.
"What? The club pay for all this?"
"Yes, a little perk for the board. Drinks and food after a board meeting. You guys put the time and money in, so Mr Spence likes to treat you. Either the club pays or the chairman sorts it out, out of his honorarium."
"He gets an honorarium?" asked Nigel, incredulously.
"Yes that's what he likes to call it, but keep that to yourself," said Simon.

The more Nigel heard, the more confused he became. He felt he'd learnt nothing at the meeting and contributed even less. He hadn't hit it off with anyone there, and he realised he desperately needed to impose himself more. Only Simon, revealing the last snippet of information, gave him some hope that he might have an ally.
"Simon, I need to get some sort of handle on how things work at the club. Can I come and see you in the next couple of days?" he asked.
"Of course, Nigel. Just give me a ring," replied the secretary.

Nigel went over to Jake and Alfred who were deep in conversation. They ignored him as they carried on talking. Nigel decided he would stay put, even though they were discussing the chairman's demand for more investment.
"What can I do, I love the bloody club," said Jake, undeterred by Nigel's presence.
"Out of order though," said Alfred. "A deal's a deal. Threatening to change the articles is a bit rich. I put my brass in in good faith."
"I'll probably sell the villa. We never use it anyway," said Jake.
"Interesting meeting gentlemen," interjected Nigel. "A lot to take in."
"What? Oh yes. Another glass, Jake?" said Alfred. "Look Day, I'm not going to beat about the bush. I didn't agree with you joining the board. We've got a good little team here, and we work together well. Your father buying shares swung it, because we need the money. And now you're with us, I'll accept it and we'll make the best of it. You're going to need to do your bit though, don't forget that. Ah, here's the grub, come on Jake, let's get in first before that gannet of a chief exec swoops on it."

Nigel was left standing on his own, as Booth and Keys moved over to the buffet that had been brought in by the staff. He couldn't believe how the two men he'd just spoken to were with one breath upset about how they'd been treated by the chairman, and were then dismissive of him as a new director.

"Having fun Nigel?" said a voice behind him, and Nigel turned to see Rick Knight walking up to him, smiling.

"Not sure if 'fun' is the word," he replied.

"Welcome to the asylum, mate. You and I have got things in common."

"How do you mean?"

"Well, Spence will do anything to raise money. The board have comprised the same group of blokes for years, but now he's desperate so he's opening it up. The trust have raised loads to get a supporter on the board, once he gave in and accepted the idea. Then your dad's thing cropped up. So you and I are the new guys on the block," said Rick.

"Yes, I read in the press you'd joined the board. Were you as confused as I am?" asked Nigel.

"I still am, mate. Still am. I'll have to discuss it with the trust lot, but I can't see me staying involved for much longer. They'll not be happy but I can't stick with something when I'm not allowed to know what's going on."

"Won't the staff fill you in? If you don't get on with the directors surely Neville should tell you how things stand."

"Neville? Don't make me laugh. The chairman runs the club and Neville does exactly as he's told. That and ripping off anyone and anything he can. The rest of them?" he said gesturing over to the group of men standing in the bay window. "They're in it for the ride. They love it, but they haven't got a bloody clue what goes on. They're arseholes."

"What about the vice-chair? Fred seems OK."

"What - you mean the director who isn't a director?"

"What do you mean?" asked Nigel.

"He's a director of his own company. But 'cos this shower are making a pig's ear of the club, he got worried, so good old Bill got him to deregister as a director with us at Companies House. That way he won't get into trouble with his own company for what he's been involved in here. All the fans think he's a director, but he ain't. Anyway, as soon as he can get his loans back, he's off. He told me that when he'd had one too many after the last board meeting," explained Rick.

"Good god," said Nigel, feeling dazed. "I'm going to have to go Rick. Thanks for the information."

Nigel said thank you and goodbye in the general direction of the men gathered around the chairman, and left the bar. In the foyer, he rang his mother. She sounded emotional when she heard his voice and said she wondered why he hadn't called her back. He felt guilty but didn't reveal he'd been in a meeting all afternoon. Outside, he hailed a taxi back to the football ground. From there he drove to his mother's house and he spent a couple of hours with her. He decided against telling her what his father's inheritance had introduced him to.

Nigel spent the rest of the week catching up with work. Sam, despite his protests at being left on his own, had done a sterling job at the Trevis house, and two quotes had been accepted for jobs that would need to be started next month. There might be a recession, but he was pleased he'd got a good name, and enquiries were coming in as often as ever. He went to his mother's place a couple of times, where he mowed the lawn and stripped the wallpaper in the hall ready for redecorating. He and Di went out for a drink to the local, and he was congratulated by some of the regulars on his new job at the club. The landlord asked him about the new player they'd signed from Spurs. Nigel had told Di things at the club were complicated and difficult to take in, but he didn't let on that he was worried. He didn't think she'd want to hear that something that was supposed to be a pleasure and a privilege was turning out to be quite different. He hoped his meeting with Simon Wall would lift his spirits and he would find out something positive about the club. Di told him that Gerry and Madge, her brother and sister-in-law, were coming over tomorrow night for dinner. Nigel said it would be nice if his mother could join them, but Di said she'd rather she didn't.

• • •

On Friday evening Di was upstairs getting ready when Gerry and Madge arrived. Nigel took them into the lounge and poured them each a glass of wine. The four of them met quite often and enjoyed each others company. A couple of times they'd gone on holiday together. When Nigel first met Gerry he was put off by his extrovert nature, and when he nicknamed him 'Too-Nice Nigel', he couldn't see them becoming close friends. Gerry explained that this was only said to reflect his brother-in-law's kind personality, but he stopped saying it when Madge told him off. Gerry was a local builder who used to own a much bigger development company that went under a few years earlier. No one really felt that it was any fault of Gerry's because he had been badly deceived by a partner who had filtered away massive sums into other failing companies, and he was very much a victim in the whole process. Since then, he had worked on smaller projects, and employed only a couple of men.

"How's life in the fast lane?" asked Gerry, over dinner.
"In the where?" Nigel replied.
"Don't come over all evasive. Some clubs have Russian owners. Some have Arabs. You'll be ploughing all your hard-earned cash into City now. Chasing the dream."
"You know that's not the case, Gerry. I'm going to try and play a part, but I need to get to know the ropes first," said Nigel.
"Yeah, 'course you have. Don't get tempted and become one of those chairman/managers. There's been a couple of them in the last few years," said Gerry, laughing loudly. "As if they know anything about football."
"Being a director will be enough for now."
Gerry then asked Nigel if he'd come round to their house and look at another landscaping job he wanted, and Nigel said he'd probably nip round on Sunday morning. He'd done these jobs before for Gerry and Madge, and Di scolded him for not asking for payment each time. He'd built a couple of brick planters, laid a lawn, and put up a summerhouse. Rather than ask if they could settle up, Nigel asked Gerry each time if he'd be able to do some alterations at the cottage, but he always ended up saying he'd love to but he was far too busy. On hearing Nigel agree to look at this latest job, Di gave him a stern stare unseen by the others as she stood up and took their plates back into the kitchen.

Later on, the two men sat in the conservatory sharing a bottle of malt whisky. Di and Madge were in the lounge drinking wine and their husbands smiled as they heard them giggling away. They chatted about their work, the recession, and the subject of football cropped up again.

"You're in the know when it comes to director's responsibilities and all that, Gerry. Can I ask you a few questions about that sort of thing?" asked Nigel.

"'Course you can old son. A building company isn't exactly Man United, but there are some things that apply to both. Fire away."

"Don't let on about any of this. Not to Madge because she'll tell Di, and I don't want her wondering what I've got into. I heard a lot of things that worried me the other day. For instance, one of the guys there is called a director but he's not. Not officially. Still says he is in the programme."

"Not on, old son. If you act like a director, you take on the responsibilities of one. Can't have your cake and eat it," said Gerry.

"And the finances of the club aren't clear. No proper monthly accounts. Just the say-so of the chairman," said Nigel, as he poured out another large measure of whisky into each glass.

"What sort of bloody shooting match have you got yourself into, old son?" asked Gerry, loudly.

"Shush Gerry, keep it down! I don't know. Every time they said something about bits of one-off income, the chairman said call it a donation. Save on VAT. And they're getting rid of the stadium guy. Making him redundant, even though he's good at the job. Got a guy the chief exec knows lined up for the job. He says he'll do more hours on less money."

"What?" said Gerry. "Not allowed mate. None of that."

"And what on earth," asked Nigel," is a bloody 'contra'?"

"Ha, well that's OK. Classic football deal that. Where you swap stuff. You know, like you get your stand done up and give away sponsorship and what-not in return."

"Oh right," said Nigel, who added in his slightly drunken state, "You know what. I wish my dad had donated his money to the bloody dog's home," and Gerry roared with laughter.

The next morning, Nigel and Sam met at a property on the edge of town, and they spent a couple of hours setting out a new terrace

and flower beds. Afterwards, Nigel dropped Sam at his local. He spent every Saturday lunch there drinking and playing cards with his mates. Sitting in the truck, he rang Neville's mobile to check the arrangements for getting access to the boardroom that afternoon for City's home match against Swindon. It would be his first time as a director at a game and he wanted to make sure he knew where to park and how to get in to the main stand. There was no reply, so he left a message. Neville had said at the board meeting that everything would be arranged for him for Saturday, so Nigel wasn't unduly worried. Then he drove to his mother's house for a flying visit before he went home to get ready and leave for the ground in good time. As soon as he walked in he realised that he'd forgotten to warn her that he would only be able to call round for a few minutes. She seemed disappointed, and he realised why when he saw the food she'd prepared for them both laid out on the table.
"Sorry mum, I need to get to the match early," he explained.
"That's OK, dear," she said, picking up the plates. "You always have lunch here on a Saturday. You didn't say."
"I know. I'll make it up to you. Take you out for lunch in the week," he said.

Half an hour later, Nigel was changed and on his way to the game. As he drove the short distance around the by-pass and over the river towards City's ground, he wondered what was expected of him. He knew the directors from Swindon would be there and he assumed he'd have to help entertain them in the boardroom. He'd rung Simon the day before and they'd arranged to meet after the match so that he could start to get some sort of grasp on the internal workings at the club. At the main gate, he gave his name to the stewards and told them he was a new director. Looking at his clipboard, one of them said he was sorry but there was no one of that name on his list.
"But Mr Walker has arranged it. I've just joined the board," said Nigel, as cars queued behind him, engines running.
"Well you're not on my list, sir. If you want to turn around, there's home fans' parking at the next gate," said the steward.
Irritated, Nigel manoeuvred his car away from the entrance and drove the short distance to the main car park. He was early and was able to park his car straight away, handing five pounds to the attendant on

the way in.
He walked to the main reception and went upstairs to the executive lounge, en route to the boardroom. At the doorway, as he half expected by now, the doorman told him he wasn't on his list either. Just then Fred Goodwin arrived.
"Who's this holding things up?" he said jokingly.
"I don't seem to exist," said Nigel, "car park, now this."
"Don't get your knickers in a twist old boy. He's with me, Brian," said Fred, and the doorman stood aside.

"Is it good? Are you enjoying it?" asked Di.
"It's OK. Strange after all these years," replied Nigel, speaking quietly into his mobile phone. He didn't want to let on that he was angry at the way he was being treated as a new director. He wasn't concerned for himself, but felt his father's final act in terms of the club he supported wasn't being appreciated by the people who ran it. He had entered the boardroom with Goodwin and, as Spence sat in a leather seat in the corner holding court with a group of friends, he realised that he could have brought a guest. He knew Di would have liked to come with him, if only he had been told.

"I think it's my job to mingle with the opposition directors," said Nigel, "I'll ring you after the match and we'll go to the local. 'bye, sweetheart." He wandered over to a group of men wearing what appeared to be Swindon club ties and chatted to them about their progress so far this season. They seemed to appreciate his attention as City's chairman laughed loudly, surrounded by his associates in the corner. A monitor in the corner of the room showed the attendance as it grew in each area of the ground, and Neville and Simon paid close attention to it as kick-off time approached.
"Clever bit of kit that. How's it looking?" asked Nigel.
"Not bad. It shoots up in the last five minutes. Bloody well needs to," replied Neville, who then walked over to the bar, reached over to grasp an open wine bottle, and poured himself a glass before joining Spence's group.
"Gates are well down on what he expected. Touchy subject," said Simon in a hushed voice.
"I thought they were good. After all these years, my dad and I got

pretty good at guessing the gate each match. They've been what I'd expect this season," said Nigel.
"You're probably right Nigel, but Neville and the chairman have been a bit optimistic."
"What average gate did they think we'd get?"
"Eight and a half," said Simon, smiling.
"What!" said Nigel in a raised voice. "Sorry. That's crazy. We'd need to be top of the table to average that."
"That's probably where they thought we'd be. Another reason we're broke. Or should I say more broke than normal," said Simon. "Look, we're meeting up after the game. I've got things to do. I'll see you later."

At five to three, a bell rang. Everyone in the boardroom filtered out into the directors box in the stand and Nigel was shown to a seat next to Jake. As the match started the empty seat between him and the steps was taken up by the manager's assistant, who made notes and spoke into a mouthpiece. The teams were evenly matched and when Swindon had their centre-half sent off for a professional foul it looked like City could sneak a win. Against the run of play, the away side took the lead with a penalty but the home side equalised with five minutes to go. Despite concerted pressure, they couldn't get the winner and a late challenge by City's captain earned him a second yellow card and a sending- off.

After the game, Nigel congratulated his Swindon counterparts and they watched as his City colleagues quickly helped themselves to the hot food that the catering staff brought in. Later, City's manager came in and the home directors surrounded him, congratulating him on a good display. They offered him their opinions on the match and Nigel overheard Alfred say that he thought City were the better team, and Swindon's formation had played into their hands. Nigel felt uncomfortable because it was clear that the opposition directors could hear this conversation. He also felt that a professional football coach wouldn't be interested in the views of a sixty-five-year-old fan who, only because of money, had regular access to speak to him. He then turned around, saw Simon Wall across the room, and walked over to him.

"You ready for our meeting Simon? I've had enough excitement for one day," Nigel asked.
"Yes Nigel, we'll go to my office," replied Simon.
"Are we OK for time, what time do people drift off?"
"Oh don't worry. This lot will be enjoying their post-match tipple for another hour or two."

As they entered his office and sat down, Simon interrupted Nigel before he could finish his first question.
"Look, Nigel, let's get this clear. It's not me you should be seeing if you've got queries about what goes on here. It's Neville. That's the correct chain of command from the board to the staff. Through the chief executive."
"I know that, Simon. But he doesn't return my calls, and when I've spoken to him, he's always distracted by something else. To be quite honest, I'm not going to be pushed aside any more. My dad made an investment into the club and I've a right to know what's going on."
"That's fine," said Simon, "I'll help if I can. I don't mind. I'm not intending to stop here much longer anyway."
"Why? I've been impressed with you and, from the little I've been able to find out so far, you're well thought of here."
"I love this club. I'm a supporter. I gave up a good job and a good salary to come here, but I can't work like this any more," said Simon, "I need to move on and get a job somewhere with some structure. Some organisation."
"OK, but if I have any influence here I want you to stay," said Nigel. "Don't make any rash decisions. What's the financial situation like? Is it as bad as I suspect?"
"Look, my official job is football admin, match-day arrangements, that sort of stuff. Except it isn't, 'cos I get all the crap Neville leaves behind. But when it comes to finance, Neville and Bill deal with it. The big stuff anyway."
"But you must have some idea."
"Yeah, what I've overheard or seen on bank statements and stuff on Neville's desk. And when he's not here, I open the mail. We're nearly two million overdrawn with the bank. Way over the limit and they're not happy. We're behind with the PAYE big style and the Customs and Excise are on to us every day. You know that 'cos they said you

should go and stall them. And there are outstanding bills for loads of things."

"But what about the end-of-year accounts? I've got a few shares. Before my dad's investment that is. I get the annual accounts. They're always, you know, not too bad."

"Spence uses the auditors he used for years when he was in business. They're tame and they put what he tells them to. Bringing some of the next year's income into the previous year's takings is a favourite trick. And it's incredible what you can hide, even in the public version."

"Anything else? Before I shoot myself," said Nigel.

"You remember Tony Spence, Bill's brother? Left the board over two years ago," said Simon.

"Yes I do. Popular bloke I seem to think. Popular with the fans."

"Yeah, well, not popular with his brother. Only came on board because Bill persuaded him to. Not a big football fan. Prefers rugby. He left after a fall-out, and under the articles of association, he gets his loans back after two years. He's asked for them back and got short shrift."

"How much is he owed?" asked Nigel, dreading the answer.

"Three hundred grand plus interest. And his solicitor is taking us to court."

"Fucking hell," said Nigel, then added: "Sorry."

"That's quite alright. That's a word I use quite often here," replied Simon.

• • •

For the next two weeks, Nigel heard virtually nothing from the club. He rang Neville to arrange a meeting with him, and was told he was away for a few days. The call wasn't returned. The only information he gained about City was from articles in the local paper and snippets on the local radio station. The only actual contact he got was from Simon who rang to see if he wanted a boardroom pass at Griffin Park where City played, and lost, on Saturday. Brentford were awarded two penalties and scored from them both. Nigel decided not to go because work was getting on top of him, and he could spend the time better catching up. Then an incident with Sam happened which alarmed him. On the following Friday morning, he reversed the truck to unload hardcore on to a piece of ground and he completely forgot Sam was laying a drain in a trench alongside. He suddenly heard Sam shouting loudly as he scrambled out of the trench when the back wheel slid towards him and the vehicle lurched over to one side.

"Fucking hell man, what are you doing?" Sam shouted.
Nigel, shaking, could only mutter about not thinking.
"No, you've been fucking miles away this last few weeks. We've got a good little business here but it ain't enjoyable any more. Ask Trevis. He's been cheesed off that his job ain't finished. Not that you've noticed. I should go and work for my uncle - he keeps asking me. If it's that fucking football club, you should pack it in. You've only been there five minutes but it's fucked you up," ranted Sam.
"It wasn't my choice, Sam, and now I'm involved I can't just drop it," said Nigel, "I never thought it would affect my own business."
"It hasn't, it's affected everything else too. You haven't visited your mum for over a week. And when she rings you look at your phone, say it's her, and say you'll ring her later. Which I bet you don't. You've been like a bear with a sore cock. Even your missus says you've been a pain."
"So you've been speaking to Di about me?" asked Nigel, offended.
"There you go. Getting a shit on again. We're CONCERNED about you, you arse. Now move that fucking wagon and let me get on."

Driving home that afternoon, Nigel stopped off to get a local paper. Back in the lorry he scanned the sports stories. On the inside page, away from the usual manager's quotes, players' injuries updates, and ticket news for City's FA Cup second round tie at non-league Hyde United, was an article that caught his eye. 'Ex-Chief Executive takes City to Tribunal ' said the headline. The article described how Walker's predecessor was taking the club to an employment tribunal, claiming his departure amounted to constructive dismissal. It went on to say that he had no proper contract, no terms and conditions, and he was forced out by the chairman, who hired him and then fired him weeks later without any warning. The article concluded by saying that the individual wanted the tribunal to rule that his dismissal was unlawful and, if they did, he would be seeking substantial damages. Nigel folded the paper and put it down on the passenger seat. Enough is enough, he thought, and he started the engine and drove home.

"This is a nice change," said Di, as Nigel handed her a glass of wine.
"We going to have a little talk. Gerry's coming round in a minute too," said Nigel.
"Really? This sounds mysterious," she said smiling.

After arriving home he'd showered and changed and told his wife that they would eat later, but they'd have a drink in the conservatory first.
"I hate to say this," he started, "but my dad's parting gift has turned into a bit of a nightmare, and I've got to do something about it."
"Is that what's been getting to you? I know you've been down but I didn't think it was that. I thought it was your mum. I thought being involved at City would be a pleasure for you," said Di.
"Obviously, so did my dad. But it's not. He loved the club and so do I. But now I'm part of it, I can't stand by and see it run into the ground by idiots."
"Well, if it's so bad, ask for the money back. Just go back to supporting them."
"It doesn't work like that. My dad's money has gone in to a black hole. And now I know what dodgy dealing goes on I couldn't resign and go back to watching them with all that in the back of my mind," said Nigel.
Just then, they heard the side gate open as Gerry walked around to the back of the house and he joined them inside.
"Hello gang, this is a bit early for one of our Friday night booze-ups," he said. "How are you sis? How are you Nige, old son?"
They both greeted him, and Nigel poured him a drink.
"We had a bit of a chat about this a while ago," Nigel explained to Di, "and I need a bit more advice, Gerry, if that's OK?"
"I'll help if I can," said Gerry.
"I told you some things about the club, but it's worse, much worse. The overspending there is immense. The club is saddled with an incredible amount of debt. There is no accountability and they are breaking every rule in the book. Directors are either oblivious to what's going on or they're in it up to their neck......"
"Let me stop you there, Nige," said Gerry, "there's one thing you've got to realise."
"What's that?"
"Once you're a director, you're liable. Any shady practice, any tax

fiddle, anything like that - you're responsible, whether you know about it or not."

"I'm not bothered about myself, it's the club I'm concerned about."

"You're not bothered about standing in the dock then?" asked Gerry.

"What?"

"Spending money when you know you haven't got it. Breaking the law. Down to you, old son. "

"He should have left the money to your bloody mother," said Di, alarmed. "She's the big expert on everything."

"Don't go there," said Nigel, raising his voice. "My mum made a mistake. She told everyone you were having an affair and she was wrong. She heard you'd been seen with Sam a few times, put two and two together and made five. You should let that go."

"Yes. Organising your fiftieth bloody surprise birthday party, for god's sake," she said, as she got up and walked into the house.

"Calm down, mate. Look, it's simple. If you're in business there's only one way to operate," said Gerry. "If you've got a problem, first off you find out the extent of it. Then you solve it. You don't mull over it and do nothing. And let it get to you, like you've done."

"OK, where do I start?" asked Nigel.

"You know I went bust. You all know about that. Well that shit of a partner of mine ended up in Spain loaded and I took it on the chin. But I nearly survived. I got help. Top bloke. I've still got his number."

Gerry and Nigel talked about things for another hour. When Gerry left, Nigel and Di made some supper and talked until late. Nigel also made some phone calls. He felt much better.

• • •

"Are you sure this looks OK?" asked Di, referring to her outfit.

"You look a million dollars. I could stop the car and have my evil way with you right now," replied Nigel.

"Steady tiger," she said, "let's see if you still feel horny after the match."

The car pulled up at the gate and, before the steward could ask the obligatory question, Nigel showed him a pass giving him access to all parts of the stadium. This process was repeated in the executive club foyer, and Nigel and Di walked though and entered the boardroom. He made sure she had got a coffee, whispered the names of the people in there to her, then left the room. Di recognised the chairman from his painting on the wall and went over and introduced herself.

"Well, my dear, I knew Nigel must have got something to offer. Now I see why," he said, hardly managing to disguise his glances at her cleavage. "Where is the old dark horse?"

"Never mind all that flannel, Mr Spence…… or Bill. Yes I'd rather call you Bill. He's meeting the chairs of the supporters' club and the trust. Introducing himself. Which is exactly what you should be doing to your guests over there," she said gesturing towards the Bristol Rovers contingent in the opposite corner. "Same with your colleagues here. You're ambassadors for the club. You should be out thanking your sponsors and meeting the fans too."

Jake and Alfred sheepishly moved over to their Bristol counterparts just as Nigel re-entered the boardroom.

"Introduced yourself, Di?" he asked.

"Yes, just as I said I would," she replied. "How did your meeting go?"

"Fine, they were pleased to meet someone from the board. I said I'd set up a fans' forum with the manager and Rick Knight. They've never had one before. The chairman, too, if he'll come. Which he should but probably won't. We'll see. If not I'll sit in on it."

"Good for you," said Di.

They enjoyed the game and City really turned it on. They took the lead when their teenage centre-half headed in an in-swinging corner, and made it two just before half-time when a free kick was deflected past the Rovers keeper. The away side pressed in the second half but City defended well. When the two strikers swapped a one-two on the edge of the box and City's leading scorer slid the ball home for a 3-0 lead they knew the points were in the bag.

"I never knew it could be as much fun as this," Di said as they left their seats after the final whistle. "I should have come with you more

in the past."
"Well, we're involved with what goes on here now. So you'll come to every match with me," said Nigel.
In the boardroom, Di helped herself to food and Nigel went up to Spence.
"Good win, chairman. Shame about the gate," he said.
"What do you mean?" he asked.
"A good attendance bearing in mind not many from Bristol. Over six thousand. Not enough for the finances though?"
"I don't know what you mean," said Spence angrily, "and I think you're getting a bit above yourself. You and your pushy wife. I run things here remember."
"I've called a special meeting of the board. Simon's got the details. He'll contact you. Next Wednesday morning. I suggest you and your friends come along," said Nigel, who couldn't conceal a smile at Spence's crimson face. Then he went over to Di and joined in the conversation she was having with the manager.

• • •

On Monday morning, Nigel met Sam at the Trevis property. They had to tidy up and sort out finishing touches before the job was at last complete. Nigel rang Mr Trevis from his mobile phone and asked if he'd like to join them in the garden.

"We've got this edging to do and I need to stain that decking. We'll take away that rubbish and then we're done," said Nigel. "I'm sorry the job's overrun. I'll make allowance for that on our final invoice."
"No, that's fine, Nigel," said Trevis. "We're very happy with what you've done. We were a bit worried at one stage, but, all in all, you've done a good job. Just like you and Sam always do. By the way, Sam told me the other day you'd joined the City board."
"Yes, it's been an eye opener."
"I bet. It was when I played there. Long time ago, mind."
"You played for City? Excellent. I didn't know that," said Nigel, viewing his client in a new light.
"Oh yes. Four seasons, mostly in the reserves. Then I broke my leg. Never the same after that."

"Well, I'm impressed you were with the club, Mr Trevis. I'll definitely give you a discount now," joked Nigel.
"No you won't," said Trevis," but you can take me to a game. Now I know you're involved, I'd like to do that."
"It's a deal," said Nigel.

Trevis left them to it and his wife brought them tea and sandwiches an hour later. At around two, Nigel told Sam he was going to leave him to finish off, explaining that he'd got a meeting in Sheffield.
"Here we go again, more bloody football business no doubt," said Sam. "Leaving me in the bloody lurch."
"It's not like that Sam," said Nigel, "not like that at all. I'll see you in the morning."

Nigel and the man with him waited in the shadows at the far end of the executive club. It was Wednesday morning and Nigel had been on edge since he woke up. They chatted until ten o'clock when they saw Neville and Simon enter the boardroom, followed by Jake, Alfred, and Rick. Some fifteen minutes later, they heard footsteps in the stairwell as Bill and Fred arrived. Nigel was relieved they had all turned up, and he invited his guest to follow him in there.

"I don't know what this is all about but I'm not having it," said Spence. "Look Day, we're due to have a board meeting next week, and whatever rubbish you want to bring up can wait 'til then. I'm only here because I need to see Neville about some urgent matters. So I'm going to leave you to…"
"OK, hold it right there," said Nigel, nervously. "I'm a director of this company and I'm entitled to have my say. And call you all round the table if I believe it's necessary. And from my short stay here, and from what I've been able to find out, it certainly is."
"I'll give you five minutes, then I'm off. You too Neville," said Spence.
"Right, gentlemen," said Nigel, ignoring the chairman. "Like my dad was until he died, I'm an ardent supporter of this football club. I care about this place. I've been given a chance to contribute to the running of the club - a chance I never thought I'd have, and I'm not going to stand by as it goes to the wall."

"What on earth are you going on about? Go to the wall? Have you lost your senses man?" said Goodwin.

"Thank you for your contribution, Fred," said Nigel. "You've reminded me of the first thing we need to sort out. I'd like to introduce you all to Mike. Mike Illingworth. He's an insolvency practitioner. The other day I had a long meeting with him. Over to you Mike."

"Thank you, Nigel. "said Mike, as he stood up to address the men around him. "First and foremost, I'm going to have to ask you to leave, Mr Goodwin. This is a meeting of directors, and you are not a director."

"What the hell do you mean?" asked Jake.

"Mr Spence and Mr Goodwin have arranged for your vice-chair to be absolved of his responsibilities but still enjoy the title. And the benefits. It seems you are not aware. Until I'm told otherwise, I'm here at Nigel's request to advise you, and I am not prepared to discuss company business with just anyone."

"You can take a running jump, now get… ," started Goodwin.

"No, that's enough Fred," said Alfred. "I didn't know you'd been up to that sort of thing. I think you'd better go. I want to listen to Mr. Illingworth. This sounds serious."

Muttering his protests, Goodwin left the room.

"And you, Mr Walker. You too," said Mike. "I don't want any staff here. Especially you, I have to say. On second thoughts, I'd like you to stay, Simon. You've been very helpful so far. Off you go, Mr Walker," and he too left the room.

"I'll keep this short gentlemen," started Mike. "From what I've managed to find out you've been trading insolvently for some time. You are acting as directors illegally, and your football club is a month, possibly two weeks, from bankruptcy."

"I knew it," said Rick, "I bloody knew it."

"You have adopted some very sharp practices, and you could easily be held to account by the courts and the football authorities. The club debt is unsustainable and you have loans to repay that you have no hope of honouring."

"I never knew things were this bad," said Jake. "What the hell have you and Walker been up to?" he asked Spence. "What about administration Mr Illingworth?"

"Hold on, I'll answer that," said Nigel. "That's not an option. We're not letting down our suppliers, our fans. We're not dodging debts."
"You don't have that choice gentlemen," said Mike. "I couldn't support your application for administration to the High Court. It wouldn't be granted. You need an exit strategy for that route out of the mess you're in. As of now, you haven't got one."
"Can I ask a question?" asked Alfred anxiously.
"Of course, sir. That's why I'm here," answered Mike.
"Our beloved chairman over there. The man who runs the club with his crony and won't let us anywhere near. I heard he takes a little honorarium for all his efforts, as he calls it. How much is this little perk?"
"Between one eighty and two hundred thousand pounds a year, from what I can see from bank statements. Possibly more."
"What ! You bastard," exclaimed Alfred, standing up and directing his anger at Spence. "You get Jake and me to put in more money, even though we've got an agreement, and all the time you're lining your bloody pockets!"
"I think we need to find time to calm down and reflect on things, gentlemen," said Mike. "If you want me to help, I will. You need to move fast. But I can't promise anything. Things may be too difficult."
Spence stood up and walked to the door. "As far as I'm concerned you can do what you like. All of you," he said. "I've run this club for years and we've always sailed close to the wind. Peaks and troughs. People in this town wouldn't let us go under. There's always a way. And I'm entitled to expenses. I don't need prats like him telling me what to do."
With that he left the boardroom.
"Gentlemen, I think we need Mr Illingworth's help," said Nigel. "Can I have a show of hands to tell me if you agree."
The remaining individuals all raised their arms.
"Mike, we'd like you to stay for a couple of days and help us out. We'll reconvene on Friday morning," said Nigel. "Simon, you can help Mike get all the information he needs. Ten o'clock Friday, gentlemen."

Nigel felt relieved that at last the club were doing the right thing. But he also felt almost physically sick at the thought of the financial situation being so bad it could not be solved. Mike had warned him that if they failed to find a way out of the mess they were in, they would have to put the club up for sale. It could leave the way open for all manner of property developers or asset strippers coming in offering the world and giving nothing. Nigel was learning fast and he had two further meetings with Mike so that they could both discuss what could be done, but, deep down, he felt helpless. Mike told him briefly about some of the clubs he had acted for and the ways they had survived against all odds. Nigel was pleased the club had hired someone with Mike's skills, but each account of his experiences elsewhere only confirmed to him how dreadful things were at his own club.

• • •

Nigel's mother fussed around him when he called round after work the next day. He really wanted to get home and ring Mike before the meeting next morning but he felt he had to spend some time with her. She made tea and repeated all the things she'd told him when they last spoke, but he didn't mind. She was bearing up well and seemed to be coming to terms with things. She had an old friend who called round now and again and they were planning on going on a coach trip together. It was only when Nigel asked how she coped at night that he saw how fragile she was and how almost frightened she seemed. Clearly, she hated being in a big house on her own at night, and no number of security lights and locks on the doors would make her feel safe. She asked again about his role at the football club and if he was enjoying it. He didn't dare tell her the truth. He said the club had got some fine young lads playing in the first team and it was a privilege to be able to talk to the manager about them.

The next morning, Nigel arranged for coffee and sandwiches to be provided in the boardroom. He knew they were in for a long meeting. As expected Spence didn't turn up, and when Nigel rang his house there was no reply. On Wednesday evening, he had told Neville Walker to take a few days holiday. He chatted to Simon, and when Mike arrived he set out his papers in front of him. Jake, Alfred and Rick then came in and they sat there looking anxiously at Mike.

"OK, we'll begin," said Nigel. "I've had some discussions with Mike and we've got some proposals."

Mike began a long description of the steps the club could take. He said they should meet the bank and come clean. Same again with the Revenue and Customs and Excise. The pro-football budget would be cut where possible this season. Overnight stays would be a thing of the past and the squad would be reduced by paying off players or loaning them out. Next season's budget would be cut by 30%. The manager would be instructed to go all out for a prestige friendly at the start of next season. He'd also be told to circulate all clubs about their best young players, including the centre-half, and accept any offer that was anywhere near approaching reasonable. A player who had been wrongly sacked for misconduct to get him off the wage bill would be re-instated. That would stop the spiralling legal costs defending their unreasonable action. Mike told them that he'd already spoken to Stoke about a keeper they'd bought from City last season. The club received ten thousand pounds for every ten games he played. Although he was only second or third choice, Stoke had agreed to pay ninety thousand pounds to avoid a possible overall debt of one hundred and twenty thousand.

"Sounds good to me, Mike," said Rick. "Does that lot get us anywhere near safety?"
"Far from it. Drops in the ocean, Rick," replied Mike. He then went on to explain that the commercial department should be set a target 20% higher, and all loans should be renegotiated. Mike told them that most of the loans were unsecured. If the club went under, they'd be wiped out so the people concerned could probably be persuaded to hold off.
"What about your members Rick? Will the fans help?" he asked.
"We haven't had a big fund-raising thing for a few seasons," he replied, "not since we helped replace that terrible pitch we had with our 'Sod Off' campaign. I'm sure we can help. Once it's known how bad things are."
"Well, we need one hundred grand from you. At least. Publicise it straight away, so the bank hear what you're doing. Good luck," said Mike.

"What about Bill?" asked Jake.

"That's up to you. He's deceived you. And from what I gather, apart from Nigel, who he thought would be a pushover, he's put off any new investors. That's another major element to your recovery. New board members with new investment and new ideas."

"I know of a chap who'd love to get involved," said Jake, "I brought him to a game. Bill ignored him."

"Well ring him, but only after you've decided about your chairman," said Mike. "And Neville has got to go. Not the hardest decision you've got to make, I would have thought."

"If we do all the things you've said are we getting ourselves out of the mire?" asked Nigel.

"Maybe. Probably not. Some things will take too long to take effect and someone is bound to take action against you any time soon. Revenue, bank, who knows? All those things are a start, that's all. I tell you what. I'm going home at the weekend but I'll work on any other steps you can take. I'll ring you at the beginning of next week."

They thanked Mike profusely and he left. The five men stayed in the boardroom discussing everything he'd said for another four hours, before they left the club exhausted.

On Saturday, Nigel, Jake, and Alfred travelled to Hyde on the team bus. They met Rick there in the home club's compact boardroom. Their hosts were friendly and the four men enjoyed watching the game. City won 1-0 with a late goal and on the journey home Nigel sat at the front of the coach with the manager. They talked together for the whole journey. We need to keep this guy, thought Nigel. Keeping the club afloat was the first priority though, and that was going to be far from easy.

Nigel and Sam spent Monday setting out paths and car parking around a cricket pavilion. It had poured all morning and it was freezing, but they couldn't put the job off. They were dressed in waterproofs over layers of clothes. When they stopped for a tea break in the warmth of the lorry, Nigel heard his mobile ring deep in his pocket. When he eventually got it out, he was disappointed to see there'd been no call from Mike, but there were five missed calls from Simon. He returned the call.

"You're a hard man to get hold of," said Simon.
"Sorry son. Catching up with work. What can I do for you?" asked Nigel.
"The cup draw Nigel. They've just done it."
"Oh god, of course. I completely forgot. Who'd we get?" asked Nigel, suddenly alert.
"Arsenal away. We've only gone and got bloody Arsenal away....."

SIX MONTHS LATER

"OK guys, here's your manager, he's going to say a few words," said Danny, the match-day announcer, and he handed the microphone over to Steve Ford. The crowd were on the pitch in front of the main stand and City had played their last match of the season. They cheered loudly as the City boss thanked them for their support and promised that they'd go one step further next season. Then City's captain spoke to the fans before turning to pour champagne over his manager's head. City had had a good season finishing ninth, only five points off the play-offs. Their finest hour by far though, had been holding Arsenal to a goalless draw at the Emirates Stadium before losing narrowly at home in the replay, which was shown live on television. Those two games had brought in over eight hundred thousands pounds. The performances of City's young centre-half had earned him a dream transfer to Sunderland, who had been interested in him for some time. Whilst the deal was based on him moving there in the next transfer window, City stood to get an initial fee and add-ons that would break the record for a player sold by the club.

Nigel smiled at Di as the fans chanted in front of him. To his right, Jake and Alfred were smiling and clapping their hands. Near them, brothers Tony and Alan York, lifelong fans and new members of the board, were taking it all in. Rick Knight stood with the fans in front of them and Nigel knew he would be emotional, even if he wasn't showing it. His period in the boardroom was drawing to a close and his successor had already been elected. Just behind Nigel stood Simon, the club's chief executive, and Peter Trevis who had joined City as an associate director. As the players larked around and the fans sang their songs, Danny told them that the celebrations wouldn't be complete without a few words from the chairman. Clambering past the players, he leaned over and handed the microphone to Nigel.

Much later, back at home, Nigel and Di fussed around their guests making sure their glasses were full and directing them to the buffet in the conservatory. People from the club, family, and friends were there for Nigel's modest end-of-season gathering. His mother sat in the corner of the lounge talking to Simon's wife. Sam was talking to Madge, and Nigel overheard him telling her how he was now a partner in the landscaping firm.
"Yeah, Knowles and Day. Sounds bloody grand doesn't it?" he said, "I thought about doing a deed poll job and changing my name to Knight. That'd have a bloody ring to it," and he roared with laughter.

Nigel took Tony York to one side.
"You and your brother have been a real asset since you joined us," said Nigel.
"We've always wanted to invest in the club, Nigel," replied Tony. "We always got knocked back. It's been a dream of ours. One of our ambitions since we went into business in the city."
"Well, the board would like you to be chairman next season, Tony. We've been impressed with your business skills and we think you could lead the club."
"You're the chairman, Nigel. You've done well."
"I only took the position when we were nearly down and out. I'll stay on the board, but we need someone with the right skills to take us forward."
"But you led the club out of the mess it was in," said Tony.
"I helped the board see sense. But there was only one thing got us out of the hole we were in," said Nigel. "It was bloody good luck. The cup games. The transfer. Never again should this club live beyond its means. We budget for what we earn. We estimate we're going to get modest gates. Out of the cups in the first round. That sort of thing. Anyway, congratulations. You'll be a superb chairman."
"Thanks, Nigel, you're a gentleman."
Then Nigel's mother walked through and joined them. She said she wanted to show the garage to a confused-looking Peter Trevis.
"Of course, mum," said Nigel, smiling to Di who smiled back. "She

means her 'annexe', Peter. All your work, hey, Gerry?"
Gerry smiled back and mimed sweeping sweat from his brow with the back of his hand to confirm it was hard work.
"Yes, we converted the garage to a little flat for her. She lives with us now," said Nigel. "Gerry did it. We called it a contra."

RELATIVE SUCCESS

As he waited, Darren pulled back the curtain and looked out of the window. People went about their business and the road was busy with traffic. A postman loaded his van with sacks from the post office on the other side of the road. Shell's front garden was untidy and the small patch of grass was deep and full of weeds. It contrasted with the gardens to the houses each side, with their neat paving and well-tended plants. Her gate had fallen off and was propped behind the low front boundary wall.

She appeared, walking briskly along the pavement back to the house. He heard the front door open and close, and her loud footsteps as she strode up the stairs.

"Here, here's your change. Twenty quid. I had to go to the offy," she said. "Don't ever pay me with a fifty again. No one uses those. Now get yourself off 'cos Billy's next and he doesn't like to see any of my other punters. Especially before it's his go. He likes to think it's special with me. He'd go mental if he clocked you and realised I've already had a busy day. If you know what I mean."

Darren sat down and leaned over to tie his laces. Shell made the bed while she waited for him. He sat back in the chair and looked at her. She was overweight and her clothes were too tight. As she leaned over with her back to him, her top and her skirt stretched apart and he could see ripples of fat and the top of her thong. Darren felt slightly repulsed by this and thought he should stop coming to see her. He always thought he shouldn't have to pay for it and he should either concentrate on his marriage or get a nice-looking mistress. Or, failing those, a better-looking prostitute, even if she cost a bit more.

In the van Darren checked his phone. He'd had four missed calls and, when he looked at his call history, he saw each one was from the office. He swore, thinking that it was unfair he couldn't get away with a little bit of freedom on a Friday afternoon. He listened to his voice messages. Colin, his boss, had left two. The first politely asked him to call back, and the second was far more abrupt, telling him to confirm he'd got the cash from the customer on the trading estate and to drop it in at work before he went home. He swore again and texted Colin to say the cash wasn't there. He added that he'd call back there on his way to work on Monday and he wouldn't be returning to the yard that afternoon. Then he turned the phone off and threw it onto the passenger seat before driving off.

In the pub, Darren ordered two pints. The barman made a fuss about the fifty-pound note offered in payment, made a feeble joke about the ink still being wet and said he'd only accept it because it was from a regular customer. Darren thanked him and mouthed 'fuck off' when he turned round to use the till. He then walked over to join his mate

Dean, who was sitting in the bay window.

"Here's that brass I owe you," said Darren, as he handed over two hundred pounds. "Don't dare go there," he said, as he saw Dean looking quizzically at the four fifty-pound notes.
"Cheers mate," said Dean. "About time, mind. You shouldn't let your mates down."
"Yeah, sorry. Had a bit of a tricky time."
"Yeah, not had any winners more like. You're late. Been to the bookies, I'll bet."
"Called in on the way here. One cert. Couldn't miss out on that. Got fifteen to one. Put fifty on it. It better win mind, 'cos I'll need to give Colin a lump of dosh on Monday. What you been up to this week?"
"Working, mate," said Dean "Never been busier since I went on the old king cole. Flat out this week. New apartments in Quincy Street."
"Yeah, and thank fuck it's the weekend," said Darren. "Apart from Sunday afternoon."
"Why, what's happening Sunday afternoon?"
"Ma and pa's wedding anniversary do, dickhead. You're invited, remember?"
"Oh yeah. What's wrong with your mum and dad having a do?"
"'Cos Lord and Lady Muck'll be there."
"Oh yeah," said Dean.
Then the two men rose and went over to the fruit machine, placing their beer on top of it, before feeding it with pound coins.

Darren announced his arrival home over three hours later by pulling his van into the drive too quickly and braking only after he'd sent the wheelie bin flying, spilling its contents all over the tarmac.
"You're drunk. And you've driven home," said Claire, his wife, as he walked in. "The washing machine's gone wrong. Flooded the kitchen. And you promised to take Ben to the park this afternoon. He's been waiting with his football kit on for ages."
Just then Ben walked in.
"Hi dad, we still going to play football?" he said.
"It's getting dark now. And I'm tired. We'll go in the morning. Is that OK?" said Darren.
"Dad! You promised!" complained Ben.

"Here, here's a present for you," said Darren, offering Ben a twenty-pound note. "We'll go and get you that new Man City shirt in the morning."
"Wow, thanks dad. Brill!" said his son, taking the money and turning to leave the room.
"You're hopeless," said Claire. "A lost cause. You think money solves everything. Anyway, your brother's in the paper. Setting up some charity thing for Africa or something."
"That'll get him his gong," said Darren, holding the Sun. "It'll soon be Sir bloody David. Whatever next."
"I need some housekeeping, we've got nothing in," said Claire.
"Here, I got you some money this afternoon," said Darren, holding out two fifty-pound notes.
"Fifties! No one takes them round here. What am I supposed to…"
"For fuck's sake," said Darren, as he walked out the room. "Ben, where are you? We're going to the park. It's not that dark."

• • •

Twins Darren and David Morgan were excellent prospects when they played youth football. They played for their school and for the same Sunday youth team. Darren played in central midfield and David was an out-and-out striker who thrived on converting the chances his team created. In one season, he scored over sixty goals in twenty league games. People knew that it was Darren's guile that set up most of his brother's goals. Most of them were easy to take, because of Darren's skill at beating one opponent after another and laying the ball off.

However, on the fateful day that the scout from the local Football League club came to watch, it was only David he chose for their centre of excellence. People were surprised and thought it would be just a question of time before he returned to sign Darren, but he never did.

David progressed through the professional club's system and, in the middle of an injury crisis, made his first-team debut at the age of sixteen. Darren carried on playing, but he grew frustrated at being surrounded by less-skilled team-mates. Then he made friends with Dean who was known, probably unfairly, as the local tearaway, and they got themselves into one scrape after another.

On his eighteenth birthday, David was transferred to Manchester United. At the end of his first full season he was a substitute when they won the European Cup final in Milan. The following campaign he became a regular in the team, as well as a regular in the Premier League 'leading scorers' chart. On Darren's eighteenth birthday, he appeared in court for taking away a car without the owner's consent.

Last month, David, his wife Lisa, daughter of a well known TV presenter, and their two boys featured in a glossy magazine showing off their newly purchased country house and its extensive estate in rural Cheshire. Around the same time, Darren, Claire, and Ben also moved into their new home. Having had numerous jobs, some of which he'd lost and some of which he'd walked away from, Darren had kept his van-driving job for over two years. This meant he qualified for a mortgage and, at Claire's insistence, they'd finally bought their first home - a three-bedroom terraced house, two streets from her parents 'home. Hearing about his brother's imminent house purchase, David had rung Darren to tell him he'd be pleased to help him buy a bigger and better house, just like he had for their parents. Darren had thanked him but declined the offer.

• • •

Darren steered the hired Mercedes into the hotel car park and drove around looking for a space. Claire told him it was obviously full and he should park in the overflow area behind the building, but he said he wanted to park where the car could be seen. They waited with the engine running, while an increasingly irritated couple hastily loaded their car with cases and drove off.

"I don't know, what are you like?" said Darren's mum, as he walked in with Claire and Ben.
"What do you mean?" he asked.

"Look at you, jeans and a tee shirt, in a posh place like this. You could have made an effort for your dad."
"I told him, mum. Happy anniversary, anyway." said Claire, hugging her mother-in-law, and telling Ben to hand over the present he was holding.
"Thank you, Claire darling. Darren's dad's over there. Go and put him at ease. He hates a fuss, you know that. He's still asking why we had to have a party. Forty years, and he thinks we should have had a quiet day at home. We've had too many of those since his stroke."
Darren and Claire walked over to his father, as more friends and relatives arrived.
"Don't you get drunk, do you hear me," she whispered to him. "Look Ben, your auntie Josie is over there. Go and see her."
"I'm having a few," said Darren. "It'll help me relax."
"I've seen you 'relax' before," she said.

"Hello son, isn't David here yet?" asked Darren's father, as his son greeted him and sat down next to him.
"Dunno, dad. How do I know when he's coming? Maybe he won't," said Darren.
"Darren! Don't say that," scolded Claire. "Of course he will. How are you Mr Morgan? You look well, you've put on some weight."
"I'm OK lass. Been hobbling about in the garden, now the weather's getting better. I'll never get used to not working. If I hadn't had the stroke I still would be. Thank heavens for David helping me. At least we don't have to worry about the bills."
"I've offered to help run you to the shops, dad. Take you out for a drink, too," said Darren.
"I can't get in and out of that bloody great van, can I?"
"No, right. 'Course you can't. I'm just going to check if Ben is OK," said Darren to Claire, as he rose from his seat and went off in the direction of the bar.

In there, Darren exchanged greetings with his uncle George. Across the room, he saw that Dean had arrived and it looked like he was already chatting up the barmaid. Despite George being in mid-sentence, Darren excused himself and joined his friend further along the bar.

"Alright mate?" said Dean. "That's Tracey. She works here."
"I gathered that mate, she's wearing a uniform," said Darren.
"First thing she said when I pointed you out was that you look like that famous footballer. I've put her straight. What she doesn't know is he's gonna be here this afternoon. Weird or what?"
"Yeah, weird. You still got that two hundred quid? I need it back."
"'Course I bloody haven't. I've got bills to pay too you know."
"Bollocks," said Darren, "that fucking horse never came in. I've got to hand over a shit load of money to my boss tomorrow."
"What you gonna do?" asked Dean
"Fuck knows."
"You should tap up your brother. What you owe would be peanuts to him. He probably tips waiters more."
"No way. I'll leave you to your new girlfriend," said Darren, abruptly.

He walked out on to the terrace. He was irritated by Dean's comments and he already felt uncomfortable being there. For years he'd hated family gatherings. Every Christmas he'd hope that they would be invited to spend time with Claire's family. His brother and sister-in-law would invite them, and Claire and Ben would say how they would love to go, even though David would only be there briefly because of football commitments, but Darren would decline the offer. It wasn't a case of him not liking David. Or Lisa, for that matter. He loved his brother. Deep down, he was proud of what he had achieved. He was proud too, that he had played football with him and contributed to his development from a promising young park player to an exciting goal scorer who everyone wanted to watch. Over and above those feelings, the success of his brother - coupled with his failure - were things that ate away at him. Ate away at him like a cancer.

Every time he'd been with Lisa in the past they'd got on well. She was wealthy, and she was at ease in the public eye. But she was equally at ease at a family knees-up. Darren usually enjoyed making her laugh and flirting with her. Several times he'd actually thought, although he'd never tried it, he could persuade her to meet him and sleep with him. He thought, however crazy an idea it might be, that maybe she'd like to do it with a working-class bloke for a change. What he felt about her wasn't lust though. If it happened, it would mean, however much he liked David, he'd have achieved something powerful over him. He really didn't want to do it, and he certainly didn't want David to find out. He'd just know, deep down, that when some idiot said for the millionth time that his brother was fantastic and - either by inference or, worse, in straight words - he wasn't, he'd know he done something that gave him some sort of superiority.

Just as Darren re-entered the function room, everyone's attention turned to the couple entering the room. Although no one moved, the whole focus of the room was transferred from amongst themselves to the far corner. Darren found himself, like the others, looking across at David and Lisa, who smiled and greeted everyone gathering round them.
"Scruffy or what, George?" he said to his uncle, standing alongside him.
"You what, son?"
"Jeans, tatty tee shirt, stubble. He looks a right scruff."
"That gear probably cost thousands, lad. Anyway, good on him getting here. United are in Rome on Tuesday. He maybe got special permission off Sir Alex."
"Yeah, either that or he's been dropped," said Darren, as he tapped his nose and nodded in the direction of the gents toilets to Dean, who stood nearby. Darren then picked up a glass of red wine from a table and, making sure no one indicated it was theirs, swallowed it in one before walking over to the cloakroom.

"Hurry up, this is a bit public," said Dean, as Darren carefully spread out the powder on the cystern lid.
"Don't fret," said Darren as he inhaled some through the rolled fifty-pound note. "They're all sticking their noses up Dave's tanned arse. Your turn."
"Hey, I'm in with that bird. Still got the old charm. I haven't paid for a drink yet. She keeps topping my glass up for free. What an afternoon, I've pulled and I'm getting rat-arsed for nothing."
"Yeah, and I'm having a whale of a time. Fucking not. The sooner I get out of here, the better."

Darren went over to Claire and Ben and sat with them. She ignored him as she carried on talking to the couple sitting with her. Ben asked his dad if he'd take him to see David.
"In a bit. When the crowd round him has cleared a bit. You'll be able to tell your mates at school you were with your uncle David at the weekend, son. How about that?" said Darren, smiling.
"Yeah, maybe," said Ben.
"You're going to tell them aren't you? They'll be impressed."
"Maybe."
"Not everyone has an England player for an uncle, Ben."
"Mates aren't how you think, dad."
"How come?"
"They say things. Like 'How come you live in a shitty little house then?' Things like that. So I don't talk about uncle David much. It's OK. I don't mind".
"You're a good lad," said Darren, ruffling his son's hair.
"Anyway, I like our new house dad. It's ace," said Ben.

The celebrations continued. Mr Morgan senior surprised everyone by tapping on a glass to gain everyone's attention, before making an emotional speech. He then presented his wife with a bouquet brought in to the room on cue by the hotel manager. Darren, by now fairly drunk, smiled as his dad spoke, and then went over and congratulated him on his gesture. Then he tried to convince his uncle George that he could build the extension that he'd heard he was having. George told him, fairly bluntly, that he'd hired a reliable local builder. He said that even if he hadn't, he wouldn't hand over a couple of thousand pounds cash at short notice to someone to buy some materials, even if that someone was a relative. Claire and Ben sat with David and Lisa and chatted away. Dean didn't succeed with Tracey, who quickly lost interest in him when he suggested loudly, in front of several people and her boss, that they find an vacant room upstairs.

Eventually, David's and Dean's paths crossed, when they found themselves in the gents toilets at the same time. David put his arm around his brother's shoulder as they re-entered the function room, and he complimented Darren on still looking in good shape.
"Yeah, down to hard work, David. And a young son who loves his

football," said Darren.

"Dad said Ben's mad keen. Bring him to Old Trafford. I'll sort you three out with some tickets for an executive box. Every home game if you like. Like I've asked you before. I'd love you all to come."

"That's good of you. I work most Saturdays though. Or mornings, at least."

"You are a stubborn bugger, Darren," said David. "You know I can sort you out a nice little job. I always need a go-fer type bloke. Driving, looking after the house, making arrangements. Things like that. My agent sorts all those things out and I don't need him for that. He needs to concentrate on my business stuff."

"You've offered before and it's good of you. I'm grateful, you know that. But I only want a job on merit. Not charity."

"Look Darren, I get paid ridiculous amounts. Not 'cos I deserve it; but because that's what guys like me get these days. Crazy sums. I put some away. I give some away; good causes and all that. I help mum and dad out, and Lisa's family too. And after all that I still have money to burn. So it ain't charity. Think about it."

"I will. But I want to be a success under my own steam," said Darren.

"And another thing I'll say, seeing as how I never see you," said David, "get your boots back on. You were always brilliant. Find a team and you'll get snapped up."

"And as soon as I fuck up a pass or miss a tackle, I'll get some arse of a manager or team-mate saying how I'm not as good as you. Anyway, I'll see you in a bit. I've left a drink over there," said Darren, as he turned and walked away.

Darren found Dean sitting at a table on his own. The party was in full swing and music started to play. As Darren sat alongside him, Dean reached under the table and lifted up a bottle of malt whisky, pouring him a glass.

"Where'd you get that?" asked Darren.

"Decided I'm not paying these prices. Saw a bloke going out and overheard the receptionist say his name. Ordered this for his room and told the waiter I'm a business colleague. Told him it was fine to leave it with me," said Dean smiling, as he slid it back out of view.

"You take the biscuit, mate."
"Not a bad bash mate. Saw you with your bro. You got anywhere raising that brass for tomorrow?"
"No, and if I don't I'm fucked," said Darren. "I'm beginning to panic now. Lose this job and I lose the house. Colin doesn't take any prisoners when it comes to bad debts. Let alone the staff ripping him off."
"What's going on over there?" asked Dean, pointing to David across the room.

Darren watched as his brother smiled and talked to Tracey, who laughed and touched his arm. Then they saw David slide open his mobile phone as the two of them continued to chat. Just then Ben arrived, jumping on his father's lap.
"Steady on, son," said Darren, as he held his glass at arm's length to avoid it spilling. Ben described how he'd had a great afternoon and how his uncle was going to get City's players to autograph his new shirt for him.
"He's bloody getting off with her," said Dean.
"Ssshh man. Bloody hell," said Darren, irritated. "Ben, go and find your mum. She'll get you a Coke. Good lad."
"Mister fucking perfect is pulling a bird," said Dean. "The one who blew me out. The tart."
"Yeah, and he's in the papers every fucking day acting the perfect family man. I don't believe this."
"Let's get out of here. We've downed all the scotch. Let's go into town."
"You're on. I'll go and tell Claire I'm going. She won't mind if I clear off. I'll leave her the car 'cos she'll say I'm too pissed to drive it. I'll meet you outside," said Darren.

• • •

In the car park Darren saw Dean standing between two cars.
"What you doing?" he shouted.
"I'm having a piss. Keep your fucking voice down," said Dean. "Here!" he said, throwing something towards his friend.

"What the fuck are these?" asked Darren, as he caught a bunch of keys above his head.
"Something to sort your money troubles out, mate," said Dean, walking over. "They're for the Aston Martin over there."
"That's David's car, you arse. We can't take that."
"'Course we fucking can. He won't miss it. The insurance'll sort it. He's got five fucking cars anyway."
The two men climbed into the vehicle, looking furtively around as they did so.
"How did you get the keys?" asked Darren.
"Laid in the top of Lisa's handbag. They should be more careful," said Dean. "Mate of mine'll take this off our hands. Nice little wedge for each of us."
"We can't do this, Dean."
"And he shouldn't shag around when he makes out he's squeaky clean. Anyway, you're too skint to argue. Start it up and let's fuck off before someone sees us."
"I don't believe this," said Darren, as he turned the key.

As the car roared into life, the two men were suddenly deafened by high-pitched yapping noises from the back seat. Then Dean felt the back of his head being bitten and his neck being scratched by sharp claws.
"What the fucking hell!" he shouted, as he reached around and pulled a furious writhing poodle from the back of the car. He held it as firmly as he could with both hands as it yelped loudly and fought to escape from his grip.
"Shut the bloody thing up, man!" shouted Darren.
"It's trying to fucking kill me!" retorted Dean.
"Give it here, for god's sake," said Darren, as he grabbed the dog away from his friend. With his face turned away to avoid the animal's frantic attempts to injure him, he held it out the open window and threw it across the gravel surface. Then he put the car in gear, and made to drive off.
"Typical, them having a designer dog," said Darren.
"I'm cut to fucking ribbons," said Dean, examining himself.
As the car screeched across the gravel, the dog recovered from its fall and, still furious, turned and ran back towards the vehicle, barking angrily. Darren concentrated on finding the exit while Dean watched

to see if anyone had seen them. Then the men noticed that peace and quiet suddenly resumed at exactly the same time as they felt the vehicle lift and descend over a small, soft obstruction.
"Fucking hell," murmured Dean.
As they drove away, they turned and looked at each other, guiltily.

Driving the car, Darren tried to forget about the incident in the hotel car park and, convincing himself it didn't matter that he'd stolen his brother's car, thought how good it felt to be in such an impressive vehicle. He was drunk and he was struggling to work out all the controls, but he fleetingly wondered how important he would look to people as he drove past.

Back at the hotel, the celebrations had subsided.
"It's such a shame. They're a lovely couple," said Tracey, to the hotel manager. "She's distraught about that dog. She said it was called Mitzy."
"I'm more concerned about the publicity," said Bernard.
Through the window they could see a police constable earnestly standing on guard next to the small body which was covered with a hotel tea towel. Across the room, in the corner, another policeman interviewed David as his wife sat nearby being comforted by his mother and father. Most of the guests had left.
"He even gave me the number of his wife's hairdresser earlier," said Tracey, "so down-to-earth. Not what you'd expect."
"My god! There's someone here with a camera now," said Bernard, "they don't bloody hang about."

• • •

Darren and Dean walked into the snooker hall and ordered double whiskeys at the bar. The click of snooker balls punctuated the silence in the dimly-lit room. The only other background noise came from a small television fitted on a bracket, high on the wall above the optics.
"Where the fuck is Toddy?" said Dean, as he gestured to the steward to pour them more drinks.
"Another of your reliable mates," said Darren. "He needs to hurry up, I'm fucking shaking after all that."

"Calm down, we're gonna be loaded when we've done the deal."
"We better be."
Just then, an elderly man wearing a trilby hat and a crumpled grey suit walked in and looked slowly around. He gave the impression of being someone who had been affluent once - but wasn't now. Despite the 'no smoking' signs, he puffed away at a fat cigar. Dean ordered yet more whisky, including one for their guest.

"Is that him?" asked Darren.
"Yeah," replied Dean.
"He looks like a paedophile."
"He might be for all I know. I don't care, as long as he buys your car."
"It's not my fucking car!"
"Toddy. Over here!" shouted Dean. "Darren, this is Toddy, old friend of mine."
"Old friend, my arse," said the man. "You don't mix in my league, young man. What wild goose chase have you got me on, on a Sunday afternoon, when I'm happily in the bosom of my family?"
Dean lightly held Toddy's elbow and led him over to the window. He lifted the blind. After a few seconds, they joined Darren back at the bar.
"What do you reckon, Toddy?" asked Dean.
"Mr Todd to you, young man. I know about you, and you're a wrong 'un. The car's not bad, though. I might be interested."
"We need to sell it today, so I reckon thirty grand's fair."
"Enjoy the rest of your day, gentlemen. Seems it's right what I've heard about you. I knew this was a waste of time," said Toddy, as he turned to leave.
"No, hang on," said Darren. "Have another scotch. What can you run to?"
"Five max. Take it or leave it."
"Fucking five grand ! It's a hundred-grand car," said Dean. "You're taking the… "
"Shut up Dean," interrupted Darren. "Ten, Toddy."
"You've nicked a car and you need the money right now. You're in no position to argue. I'll give you two grand now 'cos I'm carrying that, and three tomorrow. Take it or leave it."

Just then Darren's attention was drawn to a familiar figure on the TV behind the bar. His brother could be seen, being interviewed by a news reporter.

"Something distracting you, gentlemen?" said Toddy, quickly noticing that the negotiations were being interrupted. Just then a photograph of an Aston Martin appeared on the screen. Then the interviewer reappeared, this time putting a question to a police officer.

"Well, I never! You're trying to sell me the most noticeable motor in the north of England. And drop me right in it," said Toddy, his voice raised as he took his mobile phone from his pocket. "I think I'll ring my son-in-law. See if he and his pals can nip over and teach you two a lesson. You shits."

"Ring who you like, you smelly old twat," said Dean, as Darren pulled him away. "We don't need your fucking money."

As Dean continued to hurl abuse, Darren dragged him out of the hall. In the alleyway they ran to the car and Darren quickly climbed in. Before he joined his friend, Dean paused to violently kick the side of the immaculate red Jaguar parked alongside, leaving it with a huge dent in the driver's side door.

"Let the old git iron that out! Fucking typical though, ain't it? Your brother fucks you up yet again," said Dean, as Darren drove off at high speed.

"We need to dump this thing. It's no good to us now. Oh, bollocks!" said Darren, by now very drunk, as he tried to avoid a commercial waste container and scraped the side of the Aston Martin along it.

"So we've got the law after us, and now Toddy's heavies," said Dean. "Head for the industrial estate over there. It's time for a bonfire."

• • •

Mr and Mrs Morgan, helped by Claire and Ben, loaded their car boot with presents. David and Lisa hugged them and said their goodbyes.

"Sorry we upset your day with the car thing. And Mitzy," said David, his arm around Lisa to console her. "I'm off to Italy tonight to join up with the squad. Not that I feel like going now."

"I'll be alright love," said Lisa, who then turned to Claire. "Lovely to see you guys today. We must get together more often. Where's Darren? Has he already gone?"

"Yes, he went a bit ago. He went off with Dean," replied Claire.

"Lovely to see you too. I'll get Darren to stop being so stubborn and we'll come to Old Trafford, like you suggested."
David and Lisa walked across the car park to the waiting taxi, turning to wave goodbye to their family.
"So Darren and that mate of his left earlier did they?" said Lisa to her husband as they opened the taxi doors. "They were pretty drunk. You don't think they had anything to do with the car and Mitzy..."
"Hell no, Lisa," said David. "That's a bit harsh. I know Darren's a bit deep, but he'd never do anything like that. Not to us."
"Sorry love," she said. They both put on their seat belts and waved once more to their relatives as the cab pulled away from the hotel.

At the precise moment David was issuing a ringing endorsment of his brother's character, across town in the grounds of a disused factory, Darren was putting a match to his car. Dean, meanwhile, was on all fours, throwing up. He'd siphoned petrol out of the tank with a piece of hose, to pour over the vehicle, and accidentally swallowed some. The car burst into flames and, as they jogged away, they heard it explode with huge plumes of black smoke billowing upwards. They left the yard and ran down the road as fast as they could, past boarded-up workshops and between rows of industrial units. Heading for the centre of town they turned a corner and were almost run over by a large black four-by-four which screeched to a halt in front of them.

"Didn't know you'd got Red Indian blood in you," said Denzil, Toddy's son-in-law, climbing out of the car, followed by three shaven-headed mates. "Your smoke signals made finding you a piece of piss. We thought you'd be thick enough to torch the motor. Predictable or what?"

Darren turned to escape, but found he was suddenly surrounded. He noticed Dean had been quicker off the mark, and could be seen about thirty yards away making his escape along the canal path.
"Looks like your mate has left you in the lurch," laughed Denzil. "Right then, down to business. Toddy only buys proper knock-off. Not dodgy knock-off he can't sell on. You should know that. And then you bash his motor."
"Giving me a panning won't sort it out. I'll give you some dosh,"

said Darren, shaking. "You can tell Toddy you've taught me a lesson, and you've made a few quid on the quiet."
"How much you got?"
"Well, not much at the moment, but I'll get it to you tomorrow."
"You're a fucking joke," said Denzil, who then gestured to his mates. "OK lads, time for some fun."
Darren took a swing as the first man advanced and hit him squarely on the side of the head. But it was token resistance, as the others jumped onto him and forced him to the ground. Then, one kick after another rammed into him as he lay there writhing, curled up to protect himself as best he could. They pummelled him for several minutes before Denzil told them to stop. He walked over slowly and lifted Darren's head by his hair.
"Don't fuck with us again," he said, as he dropped his head back down. Then the four men climbed back into the vehicle laughing loudly and drove off.

As Darren stared, Lisa slowly lifted her blouse over her head and threw it to the floor. Then she reached behind her back and unclipped her bra. He looked at her firm breasts as she gestured to him to come over. He told her to lie down. Instead, she made a horrendously loud barking sound. Startled, he looked up to see her hairy face and long teeth. He recoiled as he realised that she had the face of a slobbering dog. Then a whistle blew and he turned to escape, running as fast as he could. Somewhere in the corner of his eye, he could see another man running in the same direction, wearing the same red shirt. Lights shone down on them and the rumbling sound of a hundred thousand people grew louder and louder. The man had a bright white ball and, still running at high speed, he kicked it high in the air in Darren's direction. Automatically, Darren dived forward and felt the ball thud against his forehead. The noise was replaced by a deafening roar and as he landed full length on the wet, manicured grass he was blinded by the flashing lights of cameras and buried under the weight of a great many men. They kissed him and embraced him and he could hear them shouting his name.

"Darren! Darren! You OK, mate?"
Darren opened his eyes. His head was pounding and every bit of his body hurt.

"I came back for you, mate. Couldn't leave you."
Darren blinked as he lay looking up at the sky. He could see the silhouette of his friend leaning over him, and he could smell alcohol and stale tobacco on his breath.
"You left me. You left me knowing they'd half-kill me," he whispered.
"I thought you'd run too," said Dean. "Anyway, I didn't think there was any point in us both getting hurt."
Darren reached up and grabbed Dean by the throat. He pulled him towards him so their faces were inches apart.
"You're a fucking loser and a fucking coward," he said, the anger growing within him and giving him strength. "And you've made sure I'm a loser too."
"You've made sure of that yourself," said Dean, retaliating, "'cos of the fucking great chip on your shoulder."

Dean backed away as Darren rose and moved towards him, his left arm clutching his ribs. Darren, ignoring the pain, ran at his friend and swung a clenched fist at him. Dean stepped backwards and, ducking to avoid the blow, lost his footing. He fell across the dirt towpath and slid over the concrete edge into the canal. As he fell into the water, the side of his head hit the corner of a breezeblock lying under the surface and, as he lay there, the water around him turned pink and then deep red. Darren watched as Dean slipped deeper into the water. He heard a voice and, looking up, saw an angler a hundred yards away on the other side of the canal. His rod lay on the towpath and he was shouting and pointing at Dean and then at him. Then he put his mobile phone to his ear. Darren looked down again at Dean's motionless body, turned, and ran as fast as he could.

• • •

Detective Constable Andy Marks had woken up early on Sunday morning hoping for a quiet shift. He'd worked until midnight on Saturday evening and then stopped off to buy the curry he'd been looking forward to all day. What he hadn't accounted for however was the negative effect it would have on his digestive system, and he spent most of the next three hours on the toilet. As a result, he hoped he'd spend the day peacefully catching up with paperwork, but he'd been called out to investigate one incident after another. The highlights of these, if that was the right word, was the demise of an old schoolfriend's dog and the theft of his posh car, followed later by the discovery of said vehicle burnt out near a disused factory. And now, just when he was hoping for a discreet forty winks back at the station, he was on his way to deal with some nutter who was threatening to jump off the viaduct. As he brought the car to a halt his radio crackled in to life.

"There's a what? A body? Where? In the canal. Hell's teeth, the town's gone bloody mad," he said. "Look I can't do anything for the stiff. Send someone else. I'll get there after I've coaxed this arsehole down from up in the clouds."

Marks walked from his car along the path until the viaduct came into view. Police tape cordoned off the area and officers and onlookers mingled together.
"Get these people to move away will you," said Marks to the policemen. "Who's the guy up there?"
"Darren Morgan, local guy," replied the constable. "Lady over there has identified him."
"My god, it's Darren?" said Marks. "I know him. Went to school with him. And his twin brother."

By now his head was spinning. That afternoon, he'd seen David for the first time in years, and now he was looking at his twin brother standing high above him, threatening to kill himself. He'd not spoken to Darren since their school days, but he'd heard his name mentioned at the station now and again in connection with one misdemeanour or other. At school, he'd got on better with Darren than David. He was the funnier of the two and he was more popular. He was the better footballer too. David, however, was more dour, more driven, and didn't care as much about people's feelings. And now, after losing touch with them, he'd run into both of them again in the space of an hour, and he'd got a very difficult situation in front of him.

Marks climbed the embankment slowly, every now and again looking up and checking that Darren was still standing on the parapet. He cursed his lifestyle and vowed he'd stop smoking, as each step made him more hot and breathless. He wondered if he'd have enough breath to actually talk to him. He'd only dealt with one other potential suicide before. She was very young and he soon knew she had no intention of jumping. He went along with it and chatted to her for nearly two hours while she made sure her fretting boyfriend was taught a firm lesson for carrying on with her best mate.

Eventually, Marks reached the top.
"Hi Darren," he said. "I'm Andy. We were in the same class at school."
Darren ignored him, and remained standing unsteadily on the parapet staring forward, tears trickling down his face. In the distance lay rolling hills and farmland, as the viaduct crossed over the valley. The main line railway passed below the central arch. Far from dispersing, the crowd watching below steadily grew and Marks recognised a couple of reporters and photographers amongst them.

"Andy Marks. I was sub a few times for the school team you and David were in," said Marks, trying again.
"Yeah I remember," said Darren quietly. "Skid Marks. Spotty little fucker. Always hanging around trying to get in with us."
"If you like."
"If you're a copper, fuck off. In fact, fuck off, whatever you are."
"OK, I'll go in a bit. You want a ciggy?"
"Yeah. Light it and put it on here," said Darren, pointing down to the stone coping. Marks did as he was asked and stepped back.
"Thanks," said Darren, his tone less aggressive. "What happened to that pig-ugly bird you went out with at school?"
"I married her," said Marks.
"Oh right. Sorry."
"That's OK."
"You lot found Dean yet?" asked Darren.
"Dean? Who's Dean, Darren?" responded Marks.
"My best mate. I killed him."
"You mean the lad in the canal?"
"I killed him," said Darren, crying again.

"We can sort it all out Darren," said Marks. "Your family will help you. You've got a lot of people who love you."
"Feel sorry for me."
"You were always the better brother."
"They think I'm nothing. My dad never asks me what I'm doing. How I am. All he talks to me about is David. He's never once told me I've done anything well."

The two men chatted for a few more minutes, and Marks felt he was getting through. Although the subjects they talked about were shallow, he thought he was beginning to win Darren over.

Down below, even more people were watching. Marks wondered if it was time to try and get closer to Darren. He slowly stepped towards him.
"Stay where you are!" shouted Darren, shuffling closer to the edge. Marks quickly withdrew.
"Easy, Darren," he said. "Easy."

Just then a large outside broadcast van with a dish mounted on the roof pulled up on the hillside. Two men jumped out and started to assemble a camera on a tripod. A light shone and a girl appeared, speaking into a microphone in front of them, Darren in the background. He slowly turned to Marks, surprising him, his dark mood suddenly transformed.
"Tell Claire to milk it. For all it's worth," he said. Then he smiled, a genuine broad happy smile, stuck a finger defiantly up to him, winked, turned back to face the valley and, still beaming, jumped. Marks' instinct was to hurl himself forward to try and grab him, but Darren had leapt athletically upwards and outwards like an Olympic diver and there was no time. He leaned over the top of the parapet to see Darren falling headfirst, his arms outstretched like a gliding bird. People screamed as he fell and then smashed into the ground. At the same time the cameras flashed and whirred and captured every moment.

GIVE AND TAKE

"Are you nervous?"
"Yeah, a bit. Why? Does it show?"
Adrian had arrived early for his first board meeting and was waiting with club secretary Liz in her office. "No, not really," she said smiling. "Anyway, it's only natural if you are. You'll be fine. You'll do a good job."
"Thanks for saying that. I hope I do," he said, smiling back.

He'd got to know Liz over the last few months and had soon regarded her as an indispensable and approachable member of the staff. Those qualities couldn't be used to describe some of the others who worked there. Anyway, he thought, from today he wasn't an outsider any more, he was one of them, so it would be interesting to see if the strained tolerance they used to show changed to something more loyal. The club office had a reputation for being aloof. Many fans felt that they spent more time worrying about themselves - and what they had to contend with - than actually trying to be helpful. Of course, they never had enough staff, and, of course, they were often in the firing line when it came to angry fans complaining about ticket arrangements or postponed games. Adrian felt that they could project the club better, even if there would never be any spare money for extra staff or better equipment. He was the middle man now. This would be one of the many jobs he'd be taking on. He'd see if he could improve things. If he didn't, those angry fans would be getting on to him now.

The phone rang and Liz told Adrian that the chairman was ready for him. He knocked and entered the boardroom and was surprised to see the directors sitting around the table with papers strewn amongst them. As a fan of the club and member of the trust board, joining the main board for the first time, Adrian knew that he needed to get off to a good start. That good start had to include making sure he was involved in all the decision making, and it looked to him that some of the meeting had taken place already.

"Sit down, Adrian," said chairman John Boyd, "and welcome aboard."
"Thank you, John," said Adrian. "Though I have to say I'm a bit unhappy you've started without me. The Trust have done what you asked, raised the money, got the members, and you said whoever was elected would play a full…"
"Hold on, hold your horses, you've not missed anything," said John, smiling broadly. "The guys and I have only met early to work out what we're all contributing to the boardroom renovations. Every year, we all donate a lump of money towards something the club needs. Something we don't want the club to have to pay for. We contribute either as sponsorship or make a straight donation. Now, if you want

to put your hand in your pocket, you can certainly be a part of what we've been talking about. Maybe you'd like to buy the oak panelling for example?"

"Oh, er, I see," said Adrian, red-faced, "sorry."

"Not a problem, young man. I guess you're going to get a lot of questions from the supporters from now on. You're going to want to know the lot."

"Can I just say it's an honour to be on the board. I'll do my best to contribute as much as possible," said Adrian.

"Oh, you'll get plenty to do," said John, grinning again.

Adrian spent much of the meeting trying to take things in and not look out of his depth. The board spent almost two hours analysing the accounts, and Adrian looked at the sea of figures in front of him, wondering if he'd ever get to know what they all meant. Forecasts, budgets, monthly accounts, departmental accounts, and year-to-date figures all seemed unfathomable, and he vowed that he'd enrol on an accountancy course the minute he left the boardroom. What use would he be if he couldn't understand the club's finances?

More straightforward, and definitely more interesting, were copies of the players' matrix which the chairman handed out almost reluctantly. Adrian could soon see why. The club's maximum wage, whilst not revealed in detail, was often referred to in principle in the local media. It was used to tell supporters that the club would not overspend on wages and would only live within its means. There definitely seemed to be a maximum monthly wage, but it seemed almost every player would receive more than that, and sometimes much more, by just doing their job. Most were given appearance money, so by being picked for the starting eleven, they would get a generous bonus. The wording "named as substitute and entering the field of play" also featured a lot. This possibly explained why the manager brought on a substitute in the ninety-fourth minute, thereby ensuring a player, disappointed at not playing, had the blow cushioned by getting an extra few hundred quid. Clean sheets by keepers, goals scored by strikers, consecutive appearances in the team, all benefited the recipients by pretty generous sums. It struck Adrian that a lot of players would qualify for bonuses when the team wasn't actually doing that well. It surely wasn't too much to ask that one of the strikers might score ten goals in a season, even if the team were near the bottom of the league. According to the matrix, if he did, he'd be entitled to twenty grand, and ten more for every additional five goals. Adrian thought this was downright crazy. The more he digested the players' salaries and bonuses, the more he realised he'd have to speak up. Especially when the supporters had been told the club had a strict wage policy and wouldn't be held to ransom by players and their agents. It certainly seemed like the chairman had been economical with the truth.

"It says here, chairman, that Buzak gets £750 every time he's in the starting eleven. Is that on top of his wages?" he asked.

"Yes, Adrian. And he's done well for us," John replied, smiling at him.

"So your maximum wage thing is a load of boll... isn't really the whole story."

"There's a difference between salary and incentivising the players. Standard practice."

"Chairman, he's a footballer. He's already paid to play. He shouldn't need to be spurred on to get in the team by getting even more money."

"We need to attract players here. We only do what other clubs do. I have to put out the right message to the fans, but we've got to get the players to join us too."

"So you lie to the fans, and give the players silly money," said Adrian.

"You've got a lot to learn, young man. And I'd keep quiet and learn the ropes before you make those sort of comments, if I were you. Your position in here might be a very short-lived one if you're not careful," said John, this time not smiling at all.

As the men continued to work their way through the agenda, the antique clock on the boardroom wall chimed five o'clock.

At the same time, Nat, Adrian's wife, walked into the cafe bar to meet her best friend, Chris, for a drink. They ordered a bottle of wine and sat down at their favourite table near the window. Nat was never one to be reluctant about speaking her mind or letting her opinions be known, while Chris was always happy to listen and chip in when necessary. With Nat taking the lead, they chatted about work, friends and family and arranged a night out together later in the month. Chris then asked Nat about Adrian's new role at the football club.

"Oh, you know Adrian," she said. "He never does anything by halves."

"He's always into something, your fella," observed Chris. "The amount of things he takes on, it must make life interesting."

"Oh yes, but he never does it like any other bloke would. It's never just an interest. Whatever he does, he becomes obsessed with it."

"Come on, Natalie, you love him really. Jim never does a bloody thing."

"It's like when he decided to take up cycling," said Nat. "He has a go on a mate's racing bike with a seat that looks like it'd go right up your bottom. Next thing I know, he's bought a bike for himself and he walks in wearing bright yellow lycra from head to toe. All he needed was a label with bloody Fyffes written on it!"

Chris poured Nat more wine and returned to the subject of Adrian and the football club.

"He must be proud he's become a director. He's been a fan for years." she said.

"All the more reason he'll get consumed by it," said Nat. "Now he's on their committee, or whatever it's called, I'll never get a look-in. If he's not involved in anything, he never leaves me alone. If he is, it's like living with a bloody zombie. He never talks, he never listens. I could sit there and say I'm going to massage his body in baby oil and all I'll be wearing is earrings. Then I'd say I'm going to give him three hours of intense pleasure so are you ready cowboy? And he'd keep reading whatever he's got his nose stuck in and say 'yeah, OK Nat' without a bloody clue what I'd been going on about."

"I'll get another bottle," said Chris.

As soon as Tony, the chief executive, had finished his report, the manager, Dean, entered the boardroom. Adrian was still reeling from the volume of ground Tony had covered. The main thing that struck him was the huge amount of work the small band of staff had to do, whilst the number of football staff was much higher. Looking through the report, he could see that the pro-football department included assistant physios, goalkeeping coaches, a whole scouting network, a sports psychologist, and a huge squad - some of whom he judged had no prospect of getting into the first team. The rest of the club staff structure seemed skeletal by comparison. Maybe this explained why the office staff came over as a bit curt sometimes, he thought.

Adrian had only ever seen Dean being interviewed on television or standing on the touchline. Now he was here at a board meeting sitting next to him. Dean seemed much more subdued than he appeared in public, especially when spoken to by his chairman. Looking down at his notes, he gave a brief assessment of the team's performances that month, ran through his injury list and described how he hoped the season would develop. He then described an offer from Watford for the reserve keeper, and confirmed that John had turned it down. The directors then asked him questions about a variety of topics, most of which Adrian thought were things fans might ask, unlike the earlier part of the meeting when they concentrated on club policy and strategic issues. It seemed like having access to question the manager was a perk that went with being a director. Dean answered each enquiry politely, even though Adrian thought some of the queries were banal or irrelevant. This must be the price a manager has to pay when a club seeks investment from businessmen, he decided. Just as this part of the meeting appeared to be drawing to a close, a director asked Dean why he didn't play three centre-halves sometimes, and was this was why the team had conceded goals from set pieces.

"I'd play 5-3-2 most of the time, but I'm not allowed ….no, rather, I haven't got the personnel," he replied.

"Are you saying the club won't let you play the system you prefer, Dean?" asked Adrian, speaking to the manager for the first time.

"With the players I've got, I'm not allowed to, I mean. I mean they're not suitable for it," said Dean, looking distinctly uneasy.

"You're the manager. No-one in here has any coaching badges, I'd guess," said Adrian, looking at the chairman.

"Thank you, Dean. That's a very full report," said John. "I'll see you tomorrow. I know you're heading off to a reserve game at Forest tonight so you'd better make tracks. Off you go."

With that, the manager left the room and the meeting began to draw to a close.

"Chairman. Can I have a word?" asked Adrian.

The men were standing now, in little groups, with a member of staff bringing round drinks.

"Yes, Adrian," said John Boyd.

"I've been party to a lot of information about the club today. I'm elected by the fans, and they will be mad keen to know more about the club they support. Can you tell me what I'm definitely not allowed to talk about?"

"I'm not going to go through it all chapter and verse, Adrian," said John. "Obviously salaries, disciplinary stuff, things like that are out of bounds. If you're on the board, you need good judgement. I'll leave it to you to judge what you tell your friends."

"So that puts me in the firing line if something delicate becomes public," said Adrian.

"Confidentiality is vital. So you bet your life it does," said the chairman.

When he arrived home, Adrian got a beer out of the fridge and went into the lounge. He was shattered so he slumped down on the settee and spread out his paperwork next to him and on the floor. He decided he'd have another go at reading the accounts and was pleased that he started to make more sense of them. He'd got other reports, a summary of the playing staff contracts and the articles of association to plough through; he wanted to be fully in the know when he met the Trust board later in the week. Just then the front door opened and Nat walked in. She was singing loudly and when she threw her bag towards a chair in the corner of the lounge, it missed by quite a margin. She kicked off her shoes, sat down next to Adrian and leaned against him.

"How did it go honey?" she said, putting her arm around him.

"You're sitting on my papers! Mind out!" said Adrian, pulling various documents out from under her.

"Sorry love, I'm a bit pissed."

"I gathered that. It went OK. I can't tell you much - I'm not allowed to."

"Don't worry love, I'm not desperate to know anything. I'm not a football nut like you are, remember," she said.

"There are things going on you wouldn't believe," said Adrian.

"Bad things? Oh dear, I gather they are, by the look on your face," said Nat, picking up some paperwork as she spoke.

"Don't disturb all those, they're laid out in order."

"Reading these might be the only way I'm going to know what you've got yourself into," she said, looking down at the paper. "Funding for Players' Pre-Season Trip, this one says. Very interesting I'm sure. All

directors to donate twenty pounds per point. What's that all about?"
"Oh, that's just a simple fundraising thing," said Adrian sheepishly, "you don't need to worry about that."
"Have you joined up to this? This isn't for all the directors is it? Only the proper ones."
"I am a proper one. Anyway I had to show willing. First day and all that."
"So for every point the team gets, you all hand over twenty quid, is that it?" said Nat, her mood changing.
"Er, yeah, something like that."
"How many points did they get last season?"
"Seventy," Adrian said, quietly.
"Seventy! So if they get the same again, you're, sorry, WE'RE handing over fourteen hundred pounds!"
"We might not have as good a season this time," he replied.
"I don't believe this," said Nat loudly, as she rose from the settee. "I knew I should have stayed in the pub. I'm starving. I'm going to make some tea. While we can still afford food."

Adrian thought about the meeting and wondered how he had come across to the people there. He knew he couldn't wade in and try and find fault with everything. Equally, he felt he mustn't quietly accept everything the club did. There was a meeting of the Trust board in a few days' time and he was aware that, after all the effort and fundraising it took to get a fan elected onto the board, they would be keen to hear about issues they had never previously been party to. He needed to get the balance right with them too. He shouldn't reveal too much or too little. And then there was Natalie. It was mind-blowing becoming a director of the club he loved, and he'd vowed he'd do everything he could to prove to the board they'd made the right decision in involving the fans in the running of the business. But he mustn't neglect her.
"I've made you supper - even though you don't deserve it," said Nat, walking back into the lounge carrying two plates of spaghetti bolognaise.
"Cheers love," said Adrian.
Just then the phone rang. Cursing, Adrian went into the study to answer it. It was Tony, who said he had some things he needed to go over after the meeting. He went on to tell Adrian that the first

team had got a friendly against a local non-league team to mark the installation of their new floodlights. Along with vice-chairman Brian Coxon, they'd like Adrian to go to represent the board. He also said that the catering manager was the club licensee but they needed someone from the board to be joint licence holder, and he seemed ideal. It would only mean going on a one-day course. As Tony went over a succession of things, Adrian didn't feel he could interrupt him or ask him to ring back – but when the conversation finally ended, he realised he'd been on the phone for over an hour. Back in the lounge, he found his meal had congealed and gone stone cold. And Nat wasn't there - she'd gone to bed.

• • •

Adrian couldn't believe it. He'd gone off to the friendly, expecting it to be a pleasant occasion and good PR for the club. Literally, a friendly match. Before he left the house, he couldn't decide what to wear. Normally, he'd have worn standard match-day clothes: jeans, replica shirt, that sort of thing. Now he was representing the club. He decided a suit and tie was over the top, and settled on smart-casual. After meeting the home club's committee, he stood with his pals expecting to enjoy the game. It was OK if uneventful for the first twenty minutes. Then it all kicked off. A player from each side tangled and they exchanged blows. Two red cards. Then the home keeper caught a high ball, at the same time raising his foot to the onrushing striker, who went down clutching his throat and the rest of the players fought a pitched battle. Dean went on the pitch, pulled his players away, and led them off, telling the referee he wasn't prepared to let his players be kicked by "animals like this lot". Adrian didn't know what to do. He looked across at Brian Coxon sitting in the little wooden stand, who remained in his seat. This can't happen, thought Adrian. He stooped under the railing and walked onto the pitch. Ignoring Dean, he gestured to the players to stay on the pitch. Then he went up to the captain and told him that the club would be in serious trouble if his team caused the match to be abandoned. Thankfully, play resumed. The players tentatively concentrated on playing football, probably realising that causing any more trouble would be bad for them and bad for their clubs.

Dean had walked into the dressing room and hadn't emerged when the game re-started. Adrian knew that the manager needed to be dealt with too, so he went over to join the vice-chairman in the stand to seek his advice. Coxon told Adrian he had no intention of speaking to the manager because he wouldn't listen. He then turned away from Adrian to continue chatting to his friends. Adrian swore under his breath, left the stand, and went into the away changing room. He found Dean, who had changed and was packing away his tracksuit.

"Look, Dean, I know it was bad, but this could be a PR disaster," said Adrian.

"I'm not having my players injured in a meaningless game by shit-heads like that," said Dean, still sorting out his possessions.

"Well, I'm asking you to go along with it. Let's see the match out and I'll be the diplomat with their committee guys. There's no point in you getting grief from them and the local FA."

"You're a director. I'll do what you say. I have to."

They both left the building. Dean watched the game from the touchline with Adrian behind him on the terracing. The game carried on uneasily, but fortunately without any more controversy.

Next morning Adrian went to work and, with his graphics firm busier than normal, only had a short lunch break at his desk. Just as he was about to leave for a meeting, his phone rang.

"Hi Adrian. It's John."

"Oh right. Hello John," said Adrian, surprised.

"I'm ringing about last night. A shambles. Brian has told me all about it."

"Not the friendly occasion it should have been," admitted Adrian.

John went on to explain how his vice-chairman had described how he'd personally kept the players on the pitch, placated the manager, and resolved things with the home club's officials.

"Well, if that's what Brian says happened, who am I to disagree?" said Adrian uneasily. "The main thing is the match was completed and we haven't got into trouble."

"A word of advice, young man," said John "Don't be slow to speak your mind. And don't stick up for people who don't deserve it. You won't last five minutes otherwise."

"I don't understand."

"I've seen a video of the game. We film them for the manager. It was you who made sure the game was finished - not Brian. And you kept Dean on the straight and narrow. You did well and I'm very grateful."

Adrian thanked John and they said their goodbyes. As he replaced the phone, he felt pleased he'd gained the chairman's approval for his actions. It was early days but he was already aware some of the people at the club needed to be watched. A lot of them weren't people he'd normally associate with - for a variety of reasons. But on the evidence of that conversation, he felt he'd earned his spurs with the chairman, and if he was going to bring about any changes, it was better to be in with people like him than be at loggerheads with them from day one.

• • •

As he drove to the trust meeting, Adrian reflected on the achievement of getting a seat on the club board. Set up four years earlier, the original trust stalwarts had urged the chairman to allow them some form of representation within the club. Eventually, realising it could make some sort of sense, not to mention some sort of extra income, the chairman relented. He set them a fundraising target of £25,000 in a season and, when they fell short by a few thousand, he challenged them to get 1,000 members over the next campaign, with the subscriptions going direct to the club. They protested about having to start all over again, and he reduced it to 500. After a lot more hard work, the target was reached and trust vice-chair Adrian Fogg was elected to the board by a narrow margin. This was their first gathering since the election and his first club board meeting. The team was doing poorly and the club finances weren't great, but thankfully there wasn't the hint of a full-on crisis yet, the like of which the fans had seen many times over the years. Adrian hoped that his report to the trust wouldn't be an anti-climax after the long campaign to get a supporter into the inner sanctum.

Pete Grimshaw, the trust chairman, worked slowly and efficiently through the agenda. They discussed changes to their constitution and the treasurer confirmed the state of their finances. They talked about their recent fans' forum, including the poor turn-out, and the manager's decision to attend for only a short time before making an unconvincing excuse about having to leave for another meeting.

Adrian then presented his report. It had already been agreed that he would give a verbal one, avoiding the risk of a written account being passed on either by mistake or, worse still, intentionally. He gave them a summary of the club's accounts and relayed the manager's views on the squad including injuries and suspensions, and areas that needed to be strengthened. As he spoke, Adrian sensed that some of his colleagues were becoming restless. He'd already decided he couldn't talk about the fears he had that the chairman was having some influence on the squad, or that the club had a well-publicised wage limit that, in practice, had hardly any limits at all. The trust had invested in the club and had earned their place on the board by right, but he had to get the balance right, and he certainly didn't want there to be an uprising after his first excursion into the running of the club. There would be plenty of time to talk about controversial issues and, hopefully, plenty of time to change things that needed changing.

"This is all very well, Adrian," interrupted Danny Marsh, a long-standing trust member, "but we need to know more. Like how much is that useless bugger Murphy on? "
"I can't discuss salaries, Danny, you know that," said Adrian.
"But you haven't told us anything we didn't already know."
"I think I have. Like the bid Dean has made for a new centre-half."
"But you haven't told us who?" said Danny.

Thankfully, Pete, sensible as ever, stepped in. He reminded his board that Adrian had to be discreet and he wasn't just on the club board to listen and relay information like a messenger. He was representing the fans in the running of the club and he should be supported.
"It works both ways," said Pete, addressing them all. "We don't just hear what the board are up to. We can get Adrian to propose things that we think need doing. Like getting our fans back behind the goal in the Town end."

As the chairman went over this old chestnut, Adrian hoped that the sigh he'd instinctively expelled on hearing it hadn't been audible. The club had told them many times that the police, the Football League, the local authority and local residents had all rejected the prospect of away fans being in any other part of the ground. Incredibly, the Trust board voted unanimously that Adrian should approach the board about it. He knew he would be trying to sell something to the club that wouldn't have a cat in hell's chance of being approved. And he would have to put it across as if he wasn't an idiot or actually agreed with it. Adrian already knew being the go-between wasn't going to be easy; he just hadn't thought it would be as difficult as this.

• • •

Adrian woke up and, as Nat slept alongside him, thought about the day ahead. It was her thirty fifth birthday. Nat was never reserved when it came to enjoying birthdays, especially hers, and she always expected Adrian to come up with good presents and successful celebrations. And tonight his club had a home game. He thought back to when he met her. After a couple of dates, she introduced him to Chris who casually told him he'd bitten off more than he could chew. He soon found out what she meant. Natalie had charm, humour, and spirit - but, by golly, had she got a temper. He'd soon recognise the signs. He'd say something wrong, or do something mildly indiscreet and the switch would go off in her head. Suddenly vitriol, bad language and, quite often, household items would fly through the air towards him. He loved her to bits but lived in dread of slipping up - especially when, more often than not, he had absolutely no idea he'd done so. Broaching the subject of going to a match tonight of all nights, or more especially not being able to miss it because of his new role, was going to take some skilful manoeuvring.

He slowly rolled out of bed, opened the door quietly, and tiptoed downstairs. He found some sticky tape, wrapped the presents he'd bought her, and made tea and toast. Back in the bedroom, he gently woke her and wished her happy birthday. She sat up, sleepily sipped her mug of tea and thanked him for the gifts he'd laid out in her lap. She opened her card and unwrapped the presents. Adrian was delighted Nat liked the large romantic card and the silver bracelet, expensive perfume and clothes vouchers he'd bought her. He was delighted because he wanted her to enjoy her birthday and because, as she opened the last one, he mentioned the club were playing that night. Somehow, the switch hadn't gone off. They agreed that she'd go out and he'd meet her in town afterwards. Adrian kissed Nat and wandered along the landing to the bathroom to get shaved, punching the air to celebrate getting away with it.

Forty-five minutes before kick-off Adrian, collected a teamsheet and, with either groans or cheers greeting each name, read out the teams to the fans in the bar in the main stand. Then he auctioned a shirt signed by the squad to raise money for the trust. He went into the boardroom for a few minutes and then joined his mates in their usual place in the stand. The team conceded an own goal in the second minute and never looked like equalising. They were dreadful and were booed off the pitch at the final whistle. Adrian usually met the trust gang for a drink after a game but knew he mustn't be late for Nat's birthday booze-up, so he left the ground and headed for the town centre. Walking along, he tried to overhear what people were saying as they trudged disappointedly away from the stadium. Apart from a lot of comments about how useless the players were, he noticed that the criticisms were mainly addressed at the chairman. No-one recognised that the whole board ran the club; everyone seemed to believe that John Boyd owned it and ran it on his own. Adrian heard one elderly guy say "It's no bloody good getting a fan involved. What good can a fan do? We need a new chairman with bloody deep pockets."

Adrian soon approached the pub opposite the station. For once he looked forward to a few hours of small talk and socialising - not to mention a break from the football club. In the main bar area, it was busy, noisy and hot. Adrian could see Nat straight away. She stood in the centre of a group of her work friends and looked happy and radiant. He found his way to her through the crowd and she saw him as he approached. Leaning over, she grabbed his tie and pulled him towards her.
"We're getting drunk, darling," she shouted over the noise. "Did you win? "
"No, we were crap," he replied.
"Oh never mind. We'll get REALLY drunk then!" she said, laughing. She put her mouth to his ear. "We're going dancing later. Then I want you to make love to me all night. Even if you are a maggot for going to football on my birthday. And I'm not wearing any knickers - just for you."

Adrian felt then, even more than he had done earlier, that there was definitely more to life than just football.

Just as he decided he should fight his way to the bar, Chris handed Adrian a glass of wine, telling him they'd set up a kitty and invested in a few bottles as soon as they got in. He handed Chris a twenty pounds note by way of a contribution and chatted to a colleague of Nat's for ten minutes or so. Then he felt his phone vibrate in his pocket. On the screen the words 'John - chairman' were illuminated. Excusing himself, he left the group and found a quieter spot near the door to the toilets.

"Yes, chairman," he said.

"I've just driven home after suffering that game, and listened to your idiot trust board chairman on local radio," said John, fuming. "He's told everyone we're moving the away fans. I've had the Chief Constable asking what the hell we're up to and God knows who else moaning at me."

"Sorry, John, calm down," Adrian spluttered. "He shouldn't have done that....he's jumped the gun a bit. The trust have asked me to put it to the board, that's all." Adrian was tempted to confirm he was aware it was a crackpot idea but in the interests of trust solidarity knew he couldn't.

"Well you can tell him it isn't going to get to a board meeting and it sure as hell isn't going to happen. And if you haven't got the bollocks to stop your mates dreaming up pathetic ideas like that, you'd better think long and hard about your position."

"It was just an idea, John, nothing definite...," said Adrian, but he realised his caller had rung off.

As he rejoined the party, Nat turned her attention to him.

"I hope that wasn't football," she said sternly.

Adrian looked sheepish and, before he could even answer, she reached over, took the phone out of his hand, walked over to the bar, and dropped it into a vase of flowers. She then returned and resumed her conversation with her friends.

"Don't worry," Chris whispered to him. "They look like dried flowers. You can get it when she goes to the loo."

"Thanks," said Adrian.

At Nat's request, the group moved to another pub. Adrian rescued himself in his wife's eyes by arranging for a large bottle of champagne and a tray of glasses to be brought to their table. Fuelled by a fair amount of alcohol, he even held centre stage for a while and told everyone a series of amusing anecdotes about their lives together. As he was ready to launch himself into the best one of all, which centred on the night he drunkenly climbed up her parents' drainpipe intending to clamber into her bedroom window, unaware they'd moved house two days earlier, he heard a man's voice behind him.

"It's no good you laughing and joking when we've had to watch that load of horse shit," said the drunken individual.

"I had to suffer too, you know," said Adrian. He identified the guy as a fan who usually sat a couple of rows in front of him in the main stand.

"Yeah, well, you can do something about it. And you should, not living it up like it doesn't matter. Especially at the ground with all the free drinks in the boardroom."

"I don't take any freebies," said Adrian, aware that everyone was listening. Especially Nat. "I pay to get in. And you're interrupting our evening. Let's discuss this at the next game."

"You need to check out your stewards too. They let their mates in for nothing…"

"We're here to celebrate my birthday," said Nat, by now standing near them, "not listen to you. Go away."

"Your birthday, love? Good on you. I'll have a drink with you. And how about a birthday kiss …"

The man stopped in his tracks as the contents of a full pint of beer drenched his chest, neck, and face.

"There's your drink, now fuck off!" said Nat and, cursing at her, the supporter turned and left.

"Well done, sweetheart," said Adrian, shaking. "We shouldn't have to put up with that."

"What do you mean 'we'? I shouldn't, you mean. You and that fucking football club," said his wife, grabbing Chris's drink and pouring it over his head. "You need to go home and get dried out. Goodnight. Come on, you lot. We're going clubbing."

Nat left the pub and was followed by her friends, who mimed their goodbyes to Adrian and shrugged their shoulders. He sat down at the empty table and dried himself with a serviette, wondering how long it would take for the rest of the customers to stop looking at him. Then he left the pub and walked home.

• • •

Adrian wrote a brief note for Nat and left it on the kitchen table. He closed the front door behind him as quietly as he could and, as he walked to the station, texted his boss to tell him he needed to take the day off to attend to urgent family business. It was very early and the train was packed with commuters, as was the tube when Adrian travelled across London.

"Hi, Tim, how are you?" said Adrian as he entered the café and joined a man sitting alone in the corner.
"I'm fine," said Tim, looking up. "I'll get you a coffee."
With mugs of coffee and croissants ordered, the two men exchanged pleasantries and talked about the clubs they both supported.
"Yeah, I've been on the board for four years now," said Tim. "I won't be putting up for election next time round though. It's been good, but it's time for someone else to have a go."
"I don't know if I'll last four months, let alone four years," said Adrian. "That's why I asked if you'd meet up. I'm finding it a bit hard."

Adrian had known Tim Peters for several years. They were both keen trust members at their clubs and their paths had crossed at matches and trust events. Adrian respected Tony for his calm manner and he seemed to have taken on the role of supporter director like a duck to water.
"Well it's never going to be easy being the man in the middle," said Tony. "But you've got to stick to your guns. If you act professionally, even if you feel like you're being got at from all sides, you'll come out of it looking professional. Don't take things personally. You're representing the people on both sides. Not yourself."
Tim went on to describe some of the situations he found himself in at his own club. He said it had taken months for some of the club directors to accept him, and a lot of fans had been sceptical about a supporter being able to contribute anything positive.
"The trust have had a lot of good ideas and useful suggestions that I've put to the board," he said, "and they've had some turkeys. I've

also had to put stuff to the fans that the board have dreamed up and I've known for a fact they'd go down like a lead balloon. But it's not my job to decide."

"It worried me rigid, going back to the trust after my first board meeting," said Adrian. "I want both sides to get on."

"They will. Unless you're a complete arse, everyone will know you're only trying to do what's best for the club. Your club and their club. That's what binds everyone together. And now and again you should put across ideas of your own too. Not be a servant to both sides all the time. You've got an opportunity to have an impact on the club you love. Make the most of it. Enjoy it."

"I think I maybe need to lighten up."

"This might sound daft, Adrian, old son, but smile. Smile in the boardroom, smile when the media interview you and smile when you get shit thrown at you. Too many trust people come over all intense. And intense, boring people don't win other people over."

"A bit like some politicians, maybe," said Adrian.

"True," said Tim. "And while I'm on the subject, you've got to dress the part too. I don't mean Armani suits, but being a fan doesn't mean you've got to look like a bloody tramp either. Little things like that help you come across better. Your choice, but it's all about impressions."

Tim described a fan who joined the board of a club in Scotland.

"He could tell you stories that would make your hair curl," he said. "The chairman left, and somehow he ended up as acting chairman. The club was millions in debt, the players were on silly money and they were paying off back tax at the rate of twenty thousand a fortnight. A lot for a small club like them."

"Blimey!" said Adrian.

"Other board members left and this guy ended up running the club on his own, apart from the vice-chairman, who was in his eighties and completely deaf, and a chief executive who was desperate to leave. With all the pressure he was under, he split from his wife and was drinking like a fish. And his own business nearly went under. But he got people in and they turned the club round. They cleared the debt and the team was successful."

"Yeah, I've read a bit about them."

"The directors who jumped ship came back in when things improved. Bloody typical. And he got back with his wife. He stood down after five years and he's had to bite his lip at some of the crap he's heard about what went on when he knows the truth. But do you know, he loved every minute of it. So you mustn't get down after only five minutes when you hear what that guy and others like him have been through for the good of their clubs."

"That's one thing I've been worried about. The effect on your personal life," said Adrian.

"Your missus should realise you've got a chance of a lifetime," said Tim, "and it's only for a short time. But you should have warned her what would be involved before you put up for the job."

Travelling home later, Adrian rang Nat, who had taken the day off to recover from her birthday. His note had been vague, and he explained what his trip to London had been about. She said she loved him and he mustn't take any notice of her when she lost her temper. He asked her if she remembered throwing a drink at him, and she said she couldn't even recall being in that particular pub. He told her he loved her too and said he'd be home soon.

• • •

As Adrian adapted more easily to the role of supporter director, the weeks passed quickly. The team won as many games as they lost, his relationship with the club board grew stronger and the trust board seemed pleased with his efforts. He had a fruitful meeting with the manager explaining what the trust did and how they were keen to help him; Dean promised he'd get as many of the playing staff to join as he could. He made himself better known amongst the fans and he pushed the local media to interview him on club matters as often as possible. As well as carry out the duties that were expected of him, Adrian introduced some ideas of his own, including a competition to find the club's 'Number One Fan', and persuading the manager and his players to carry out far more visits to local schools and businesses. The competition proved very popular and visits to the club website increased dramatically as supporters nominated candidates or read who was being put forward. Adrian had confirmed that the winner would get a mystery prize and the message boards were buzzing with rumours as to what this would be. Despite being pressed many times, he didn't let on.

Adrian grew more confident at dealing with confrontation. As the 'man in the middle', he fielded complaints well, and he directed criticisms and suggestions to the right areas of the club. Pete was a good trust chair but he was a detail man and he took great delight at picking up on what he thought were errors. He constantly rang up asking Adrian why he'd said this or written that. Adrian didn't mind and kept telling himself his chairman was a good sort, deep down. He put a list of possible trust events on their website and Pete rang to query the position of the apostrophe in the words "fan's forum." He also said he didn't think it would be a success after the last one. Adrian smiled to himself but resisted telling his friend he needed to wait and see.

Adrian's problem of committing time to the football club and risking incurring the wrath of his wife eased too. He started to tell Nat about things at the club and, never ceasing to be surprised by her, was shocked when she asked to go to a game with him. She told him she wanted to try and see what he saw in it all. And he was even more surprised when she enjoyed it. Like a lot of people who judge football from afar, Nat hadn't realised how exciting being at a game could be and she loved the atmosphere in the ground. Always a gregarious girl, she revelled in the sounds and the sights. She loved the chants and the conversations she could overhear.

To make sure Nat was getting bitten by the football bug, Adrian took her across the county to the local derby with their affluent near-neighbours a couple of weeks later. They were riding high in the league and the ground was packed. Adrian got a guest ticket for the boardroom for her although, never one to accept perks, he made a donation to the trust to make up for it. The match was a battle and the referee was busy handing out yellow and red cards. The noise was deafening and a lot of abuse was directed at the away directors' area, after the chairman had said some ill-chosen comments in the local media about the financial dealings of his counterpart. Adrian looked round at Nat and she was loving it. At one stage, she stood up and turned round, and for one awful moment he thought she was going to lift her skirt and expose her rear end to the home fans - a gesture she'd done several times before, usually on a night out and when offended by something. Thankfully, she only shouted a reasonably humorous riposte to someone behind them and then sat down again. After the game, he asked her if she'd enjoyed it and she said she had, although she wasn't bothered about mixing with the 'stuffed shirts and mutton-dressed-as-lamb slappers' in the boardroom. Despite this, Adrian felt he'd made a diplomatic breakthrough when it came to football and marriage commitments.

• • •

In the function room at the ground, Adrian and a nervous-looking middle-aged man stood talking near the top table. The bar staff busied themselves preparing the room. A local television reporter and cameraman entered and set up their equipment at the back of the room. As half-past-seven approached, members of the club personnel started to arrive and were directed to the seating facing the stage. Soon the audience consisted of the chairman, directors, manager, players, coaches, physios, chief executive, office staff, commercial staff, stewards, groundsman and representatives from the local media. Each one looked mystified at having to be there and they asked each other what the gathering was all about.

"Right, we'll make a start," said Adrian into the microphone. "And first of all, can I thank you for attending. I know I've been a bit aggressive in getting you to come, but I hope you'll think it's worth it."
"It better be - get on with it," said a voice from the back of the room.
"I'd like you to think about the most important part of a football club," said Adrian "With respect to you all sitting there, it's not the chairman, the manager, or the players. You come and go. It's the supporters who make a club what it is. They are here for good."

The mood in the room was still one of irritation and impatience, but Adrian pressed on, undeterred by the atmosphere.
"I'd like you to meet Brian. You might know we ran a 'Number One Fan' competition. Brian was the stand-out winner. He follows us all over the country, year after year. He's raised thousands of pounds without recognition. And he's been to lots of fans' forums. Well this

is his prize. A fan's forum with a difference. It's time you listened to him. I want you to ask him what HE thinks about the club. So off you go. Fire away!"

An awkward silence followed. Again Adrian encouraged them to speak. Eventually Jill, a steward, stood up.

"Why do you fans complain about us all the time?" she said.

"Well, in my opinion…" started Brian nervously.

"We get spat on and abused," Jill interrupted, "and all we get is complaints."

"You get a lot of stick and you do a good job. I know that," said Brian. "But you're the first person that most fans see when they arrive at the ground and most fans are well-behaved. So a steward shouldn't tar everyone with the same brush. There's no need to be rude or boss people about. That's why you get complaints."

Then Steve Walley, the team captain, stood up.

"We give everything when we play for this club. Every game. It really pisses us off when we get booed off."

"Most fans know you're running through a wall for us," said Brian, "but it's a two-way thing. We support you more when you recognise us. Last season there were loads of away games when you didn't come over and give us a clap at the end of the game. Sometimes, even when you've won, only half of you bothered to come over to us. That's what pisses us off."

Some people nodded their heads and muttered agreement and Steve thanked him.

"What do you think about the match-day catering?" asked the chief executive. "The club get so much per head and a company runs it. It's a good deal for us but we get a lot of complaints."

"Do you get the firm who wins the deal to agree to some minimum standards?" asked Brian.

"Well, no, we leave that to them," said Tony.

"I'm no businessman, but if the food's crap, it gives a bad impression of the club. However much money you make. Do your deals but get them to guarantee it's at least edible."

After a slow start, the questions came thick and fast. Brian grew in confidence and was honest in his criticisms. He was keen to give credit where it was warranted too. At one stage, a junior member of the commercial team sitting at the back made to leave. Brian interrupted the point he was making and told him he always thought it looked disrespectful if supporters left a fans' forum with the manager before it had ended. The young man returned to his seat. Brian suggested the club sold tickets for groups of matches for those who didn't want to commit to a full season ticket. He said junior season tickets could be made available for the second half of the season because they would make good Christmas presents. When the club physiotherapist asked how someone like him could engage with the fans, Brian suggested he could provide treatment for supporters who played local football, and how some fans would relish being treated by the man who looked after their idols.

Finally, the club chairman stood up. "I want to congratulate you, Brian," said John. "This has been an interesting experience. I'm sure we've all got a lot to think about, but it sounds like we're doing some things right too. I'd like to know what, apart from us being top of the league of course, is the one thing you'd like to see happen at this club."

"It already has, chairman. A bit anyway," said Brian. "All us fans get sick of the 'us and them' thing. We buy the season tickets and we buy the shirts. We travel all over the country. And it's our club. Yet it isn't. You guys in the posh seats have all the power. You've put your money in, so that's right. But we should have a say. Now we have because Adrian is in there for us. And I've had my say tonight. That sort of thing needs to be a bigger part of the club, not just a token for the fans."

"Thank you," said John.

Next day, the local radio station and evening paper featured accounts of the meeting. Regional television showed snippets of the event. The reaction was generally good. Nat rang Adrian at work to tell him the Guardian had written a small article about it. The headline said 'The Club That Thinks About Its Fans', and Adrian was delighted.

• • •

Adrian looked at his diary and saw he'd got half an hour before his next meeting. He decided he'd use the time to write his 'Director's Diary'. This was a feature on the trust website where he described what he had been doing at the club and revealed to fans all the things he did on their behalf. It was also designed to let potential supporter-directors see what they'd be letting themselves in for if they decided to take the plunge. He often did trust work at the office and he knew his boss turned a blind eye to it. It also meant he wasn't engrossed in football matters at home so much for Nat's sake. Suddenly, the door burst open.

"I'm sorry, Adrian, this gentleman wouldn't wait," said Holly, the receptionist, as she followed the man through the door. It was Tony, the club's chief executive.

"I want a word. Now," said Tony, clearly angry.

"It's OK, Holly," said Adrian "You can leave this with me."

Tony sat in the chair facing Adrian and leaned forward on the desk towards him.

"You might not have noticed but the manager and John have been at each other's throats for weeks," he said loudly. "John makes Dean do things he doesn't want to, under threat of getting the board to sack him. If you didn't know that you bloody should do."

"I've noticed there was some tension between them," conceded Adrian.

"Yeah, and some. And I'm stuck in the middle of it all."

"What's all this got to do with me, Tony?"

"Well Dean's heard about my cock-up. You know the one. Only the board knew about it. I only put 'promotion via the play-offs' in the contract by mistake when we sold Danny Dimarco last year. It meant we missed out on a hundred grand bonus when his new club got automatic promotion. I reported it to the board, if you were listening."

"Of course I was listening. The board let you off because of all the good deals you've done in the past. And we'd got a good fee for the lad, anyway," said Adrian, irritated. "I'm still trying to work out why you're telling me all this."

"Dean will use this as an excuse to explain why he can't strengthen the team. And he'll say it's down to the chairman. Cover his back if the team struggles, and maybe get John out. Except that won't happen, 'cos now it's out in the open, it'll be me who gets the boot. Thanks to you."

"Why me?" asked Adrian, nervously.

"Because you haven't used your loaf when it comes to confidentiality," said Tony. "This has got out through you."

"I haven't told anyone."

"No? Well your missus had plenty to say about it in the boardroom the other week. Except she didn't realise Dean's wife was one of the women in there."

Tony rose from his seat, went over to the door and turned to face Adrian.

"Thanks to your gobby wife, I'm probably going to be history. You wanted to be a director, so you should carry the can when you don't behave like one. I'll leave it with you."

And with that, he turned and walked briskly down the corridor back to the foyer.

Adrian sat back in his chair. His head was spinning with what he'd just heard. In his attempts to involve Nat, he knew he'd told her some things that he shouldn't have. In some ways, telling her about one or two controversial issues had shown her what a difficult role he had representing the trust and he thought it might make her more sympathetic. But anything he'd told her was combined with a warning that she must never reveal any of it. She'd brushed these words of caution aside by saying he ought to know she wouldn't be so stupid, almost to the point of making him feel guilty he'd even dared to suggest she might. And now he'd been told that, for whatever reason, she'd ignored what he'd said and let him down. Badly.

Adrian spent the day trying to work, but all he could concentrate on was his conversation with Tony. In a few short minutes, he'd had huge problems at the club and at home plonked firmly in his lap. And this had happened when he thought things were going so well on both fronts. He had failed the trust and the club and he couldn't cope with the thought of Tony losing his job. He didn't know what to do to resolve it. On top of all that, Natalie was not the sort of woman who took his criticisms lying down. All the time he'd known her, she'd been the one who, because of her fiery temperament, would be the reason an argument started. And then it would result in him having to apologise, whether he was right or wrong. To make matters worse, this was a football issue and she'd made her views on his involvement in the club well known, even if she'd mellowed a little in recent weeks. But her mistake was so fundamental and so serious that this time she would have to be told she was wrong and this time she would have to accept it. Any other reaction from her and he even doubted if he could stay married to her. It was all about trust and it was that important.

Adrian left the office and drove through town to pick Natalie up as arranged. There was a lot of traffic because office workers and shoppers were making their way home. He pulled up near the library and waited for her. Fifteen minutes later than the time agreed, he was made to jump when she banged on the roof before opening the door and climbing in.
"You look like you've seen a ghost," she said, and he smiled weakly.
On the way home, Nat told him how shopping had been horrendous and she hadn't got half the things she'd been looking for.
"Look out!" she shouted, when the car almost hit the back of a van as it slowed to turn right. "What the hell's the matter with you? You're not with it, man."
Adrian ignored her and kept his eyes on the road. They pulled into the drive and entered the house. In the kitchen, Adrian made them coffee while Nat threw off her shoes and sat down.
"What's the matter?" she asked. "You're like a wet bloody lettuce."
"I'm in the shit. And I've got someone else in the shit too," he replied quietly.
"It's not that bloody football club is it?" said Nat, her tone becoming angrier.
"Yes, but not just the club. It's more than that," said Adrian, still quietly.
"I knew you'd let it get to you. You can't do anything without it dominates you, you useless…"
Adrian saw her looking at the milk carton on the kitchen table. He exploded.
"Here, let me do that for you!" he bellowed. "Seeing as how it's so fucking obvious how you're going to react!"
With that, he picked up the carton and hurled it through the doorway into the dining room. It hit the edge of the sideboard and exploded, milk splattering all over the walls.
"I'm in trouble because of you!" he shouted. "Because you never live by the rules you set for me. The rules you go mental about - even when I don't bloody break them!"

"What do you mean?" she said, taken aback and her voice less aggressive.
"In the boardroom. Why did you tell those women about Tony's cock-up? You knew it was private."
"What? I might have said something. You weren't there. You were waffling on to someone as usual. He was in there acting like god's gift."
"You shouldn't have said anything. Not about that."
"I wanted to tell them he wasn't as great as he thinks he is. He was flirting with me. I'm sure he was eyeing me up."
"He wouldn't do that," said Adrian.
"Why not? Are you saying I'm not attractive to other men?" said Nat, becoming angry again.
"Because he's gay. That's why not," shouted Adrian. "He lives with his partner. He married him last year. Now he'll lose his job."
"Well, I didn't know that."
"No, but it didn't stop you letting me down, did it? I told you things and you knew they were confidential. I did it so you knew I'd got a difficult job. I hoped you'd support me more. But because of your bloody temper, all common sense goes out the window. Like it has all the time I've known you. When I've had to be as good as fucking gold all the time."

Adrian left the room and went upstairs. He found a holdall and packed a few things. He went downstairs and left the house, slamming the door behind him.

• • •

Adrian found the next few weeks very difficult. He moved into the spare room at his sister and brother-in-law's flat. One evening he waited outside the house until Nat had left for a night out so that he could pick up a few more of his belongings. It didn't take him long and he collected some clothes and a couple of books with a heavy heart. Leaving home was the last thing he wanted to do but he felt he had no alternative. She'd let him down and he needed to be apart from her to think things through. During the first week or so, Nat rang him several times - both at the flat and on his mobile - but he ignored her calls.

He decided he'd have to take the lead in dealing with the crisis at the club. He was responsible for it, so it was up to him to try and resolve it. Rumours were spreading that the manager's hands were tied by the chairman, the team was badly under-performing and the natives were becoming very restless, so he called an emergency board meeting. He explained everything that had happened - including Nat's revelations during the course of some boardroom chit-chat. It was a tense meeting and he felt particularly vulnerable. He'd enjoyed his time as trust director and he was now in the line of fire. After a lengthy discussion, the board censured John who, whilst remaining chairman, was relieved of his role as liaison between the manager and the directors. Tony was reminded that his error in the transfer deal must never be repeated, and Dean was told to get on with building a successful team - and assured that interference from on high was now at an end.

The real casualty was Adrian himself. Before the meeting, he'd spent a long time thinking about his next move. He firmly believed in the idea of a trust member being on the board but he realised that he, through Nat, had betrayed their trust. In the end, he felt he had to do the honourable thing and fall on his sword, so he offered his resignation. It was accepted. Fortunately the position of trust director remained intact - but only after a heated debate. Despite all his best intentions, Adrian knew he had screwed up and the board could easily have decided to abandon it as a laudable but ultimately unsuccessful experiment. Perhaps fearing a backlash from some of the supporters, they'd agreed to give the trust another chance. Adrian, sitting anxiously near a corner of the boardroom table like a naughty schoolboy, breathed a sigh of relief when they told him that Pete, the trust's chairman, could take his place temporarily until the next trust election.

• • •

Adrian's boss, as supportive as ever, sent him on a course for a few days. It wasn't particularly relevant to his job, but he thought the change of environment and routine might help him. Adrian enjoyed meeting new people and the hotel was set in beautiful countryside. One night, his mobile rang and he didn't recognise the number.

"Hello Adrian. It's Chris."
"Chris? Who… oh, Nat's Chris." said Adrian, at first confused.
"I wouldn't normally get involved in something like this," she said, "but she's in bits. She's always been strong, but she can't function."
"I've not been too good myself," said Adrian "I didn't think Nat would feel bad for too long though. That's why I've not contacted her."
"Meet her, Adrian. It's nothing to do with me, but you two were good together. You two had something I'd die for."
"I'm in Cheshire at the moment. I'm driving back on Thursday. Tell her maybe I'll meet her for a coffee."

Adrian parked the car and crossed the road. As he entered the coffee shop, he saw Nat sitting near the window, her back towards him. He was early but she'd beaten him to it. And he was nervous, like it was a first date. He wanted their meeting to go well, but they had a lot to sort out. He sat down and they smiled at each other.
"You've lost weight," said Nat.
"I needed to," said Adrian.
"It's good to see you."
"You too."
They chatted about work and Nat laughed as Adrian described how the walls in the flat were so paper-thin he could hear everything his sister and her husband got up to at night. She asked him about the club and he confirmed that he wasn't involved any more. Anticipating what she'd say, he said he was fine with it.
"We had a difficult time. Down to me a lot of it. Most of it," he said.
"But I made it worse. I was horrible to you. Or, should I say, MORE horrible to you," she replied.
"I did what I always do - let it take me over."
"This was different. You were doing something you loved. Being part of the club was something you'd remember for the rest of your life. And you were doing well," said Nat.
"It's about trusting people, giving them a chance, allowing them to make mistakes. Give and take on both sides."
"I know now that's what football is all about," she said.
"For once I wasn't talking about football," said Adrian, smiling.
They laughed and he put his hand on hers.

The aim of this book is to raise funds for supporters trusts. For a donation to a trust of your choice, please complete the following:

Your name

Your address

Contact Number

Name of Trust (must be a member of Supporters Direct)

Address of trust (if known)

Contact name. eg. Trust Secretary (if known)

Send this voucher to:
Taboos Troubles and Trusts
6-8 Kenneth Street, Lincoln LN1 3ED

Please do not photocopy this form. Thank you!